Oliver's Story

Oliver's Story

by Erich Segal

1817

HARPER & ROW, PUBLISHERS

NEW YORK, HAGERSTOWN, SAN FRANCISCO, LONDON

For Karen

Amor mi mosse

Death ends a life, but it does not end a relationship, which struggles on in the survivor's mind towards some resolution which it may never find.

—Robert Anderson
I Never Sang for My Father

June 1969

"Oliver, you're sick."

"I'm what?"

"You're very sick."

The expert who pronounced this startling diagnosis had come late in life to medicine. In fact, until today I thought he was a pastry chef. His name was Philip Cavilleri. Once upon a time his daughter Jenny was my wife. She died. And we remained, our legacy from her to be each other's guardian. Therefore once a month I'd either visit him in Cranston, where we'd bowl and booze and eat exotic pizzas. Or he would join me in New York to run an equally exciting gamut of activities. But today as he descended from the train, instead of greeting me with some affectionate obscenity, he shouted.

"Oliver, you're sick."

"Really, Philip? In your sage professional opinion, what the hell is wrong with me?"

"You aren't married."

Then without expatiating further, he just turned and, leatherette valise in hand, he headed for the exit.

Morning sunlight made the city's glass and steel seem almost friendly. So we both agreed to walk the twenty blocks to what I jocularly called my bachelor pad. At Forty-seventh Street and Park, Phil turned and asked, "How have your evenings been?"

"Oh, busy," I replied.

"Busy, huh? That's good. Who with?"

"The Midnight Raiders."

"What are they—a street gang or a rock group?"

"Neither. We're a bunch of lawyers volunteering time in Harlem."

"How many nights a week?"

"Three," I said.

Again we strolled uptown in silence.

At Fifty-third and Park, Phil broke his silence once again. "That still leaves four free nights."

"I've got a lot of office homework too."

"Oh, yeah, of course. We gotta do our homework." Phil was less than sympathetic to my serious involvement with a lot of burning issues (e.g., draft cards). So I had to hint at their significance.

"I'm down in Washington a lot. I'm arguing a First Amendment case before the Court next month. This high school teacher—"

"Oh, that's good, defending teachers," Philip said. And added oh-so-casually, "How's Washington for girls?"

"I don't know." I shrugged and walked along.

At Sixty-first and Park, Phil Cavilleri stopped and looked me in the eye.

"Just when the hell do you intend to plug your motor into life again?"

"It hasn't been that long," I said. And thought: the great philosopher who claimed that time heals wounds neglected to impart just how much time.

"Two years," said Philip Cavilleri.

"Eighteen months," I corrected him.

"Yeah, well . . ." he answered, gravelly voice trailing off. Betraying that he too still felt the cold of that December day but . . . eighteen months ago.

In the remaining blocks I tried to warm things up again by touting the apartment I had rented since he last was here.

"So this is it?"

Phil looked around, an eyebrow raised. Everything was very orderly and neat. I'd had a woman come that morning specially.

"What do you call the style?" he asked. "Contemporary Shitbox?"

"Hey," I said. "My needs are very simple."

"I should say. Most rats in Cranston live as good as this. And some live better. What the hell are all these books?"

"Legal reference volumes, Phil."

"Of course," he said. "And what exactly do you do for fun—feel up the leather bindings?"

I think I could successfully have argued an invasion of my privacy.

"Look, Philip, what I do when I'm alone is my own business."

"Who denies it? But you're not alone tonight. So you and I are gonna make the social scene."

"The *what?*"

"I didn't buy this fancy jacket—which you haven't complimented, by the way—to watch some lousy film. I didn't get this suave new haircut just to make you think I'm cute. We're gonna move and groove. We are gonna make new friends. . . ."

"What kind?"

"The female kind. Come on, get fancied up."

"I'm going to the movies, Phil."

"The hell you are. Hey look, I know you're out to win the Nobel Prize for suffering, but I will not allow it. Do you hear me? I will not allow it."

He was fulminating now.

"Oliver," quoth Philip Cavilleri, now turned priest, S.J., "I'm here to save your soul and save your ass. And you will heed me. Do you heed?"

"Yes, Father Philip. What precisely should I do?"

"Get married, Oliver."

We buried Jenny early one December morning. Luckily, because a huge New England storm made snowy statues of the world by afternoon.

My parents asked me if I'd go back to Boston with them on the train. I declined politely as I could, insisting Philip needed me or he would crack. In truth it was the other way around. Since all my life I'd been immured from human loss and hurt, I needed Phil to teach me how to grieve.

"Please be in touch," said Father.

"Yes, I will." I shook his hand and kissed my mother's cheek. The train departed northward.

At first the Cavilleri house was noisy. Relatives were loath to let the two of us alone. But one by one, they peeled away—for naturally they all had families to go to. Each in parting made Phil promise that he'd open up the shop and get to work. It's the only thing to do. He always nodded sort of yeah.

And finally we sat there, just the two of us. There wasn't any need to move, since everyone had stocked the kitchen with a month's supply of everything.

Now, with no distractions from the aunts or cousins, I began to feel the Novocaine of ceremony wearing off. Before I had imagined I was hurting. Now I knew that I'd been merely numb. The agony was just beginning.

"Hey, you oughta get back to New York," said Phil without too much conviction. I spared him the rejoinder that his bakery seemed rather closed. I said, "I can't. I have a New Year's Eve date here in Cranston."

"Who?" he asked.

"With you," I answered.

"That'll be a lotta fun," he said, "but promise me—on New Year's morning you'll go home."

"Okay," I said.

"Okay," he said.

My parents called up every evening.

"No, there's nothing, Mrs. Barrett," Phil would say to her. She'd obviously asked how she could . . . help.

"No, nothing, Father," I would say when my turn came. "But thanks."

Phil showed me secret pictures. Photos that were once forbidden me by Jenny's most adamant command.

"*Goddammit, Phil, I don't want Oliver to see me with my braces on!*"

"*But, Jenny, you were very cute.*"

"*I'm cuter now,*" she answered, very Jenny-like. *Then added,* "*And no baby pictures, either, Phil.*"

"*But why? Why not?*"

"*I don't want Oliver to see me fat.*"

I'd watched this happy cannonade, bemused. By then we actually were married and I couldn't possibly divorce her on the grounds of braces past.

"Hey, who's boss here?" I'd remarked to Phil, to keep the action lively.

"Take a guess." He smiled. And put the albums back unopened.

Now today we looked. There were a lot of photographs.

Prominent in all the early ones was "T'resa" Cavilleri, Philip's wife.

"She looks like Jenny."

"She was beautiful," he sighed.

Somewhere after Jenny's baby fat but prior to her braces, Tresa disappeared completely from the pictures.

"I shoulda never let her drive at night," said Phil, as if the accident in which she died had happened just the day before.

"How did you cope?" I asked. "How could you bear it?" I had asked the question selfishly to hear what remedy he might suggest that could be balm for me.

"Who says that I could bear it?" Philip answered. "But at least I had a little daughter. . . ."

"To take care of. . . ."

"To take care of me," he said.

And I heard tales that in the life of Jennifer had been classified material. How she did everything to help him. And to ease his pain. He had to let her cook. But what was worse, he had to *eat* her early efforts, drawn (and quartered) from recipes in supermarket magazines. She forced him to keep up his Wednesday bowling-with-the-fellas nights. She tried her best to make him happy.

"Is that why you never married, Phil?"

"What?"

"Because of Jenny?"

"Christ, no. She pestered me to marry—even fixed me up!"

"She did?"

He nodded. "Jeez, she must have tried to sell me every eligible Italo-American from Cranston to Pawtucket."

"But all losers, huh?"

"No, some were nice," he said. Which took me by surprise. "Miss Rinaldi, Jenny's junior high school English teacher . . ."

"Yeah?" I said.

"Was very nice. We saw each other for a while. She's married now. Three kids."

"You weren't ready, Phil, I guess."

He looked at me and shook his head. "Hey, Oliver—I had it once. And who the hell am I to hope that God will give me two of what most people never get at all."

And then he sort of looked away, regretting his betrayal of that truth to me.

On New Year's Day he literally pushed me on a homeward train.

"Just remember that you promised to get back to work," he said.

"You too," I answered.

"It helps. Believe me, Oliver, it really helps." And then the train began to move.

Phil was right. Plunging into other people's legal problems, I found an outlet for the anger I'd begun to feel. Someone somehow screwed me, so I thought. Something in the world's administration, the Establishment of Heaven. And I felt I should be doing things to set it right. More and more I found myself attracted to "miscarriages of justice." And, man, right then our garden had a lot of nasty weeds.

Owing to *Miranda* v. *Arizona* (384 U.S. 436), I was a very busy boy. The Supreme Court now acknowledged that a suspect had to be informed he could be silent till he got a lawyer. I don't know just how many had been previously hustled off to judgment—but I suddenly was angry for them all. Like LeRoy Seeger, who already was in Attica when I got his case through Civil Liberties.

Lee had been convicted on the basis of a signed confession deftly (ah—but legally?) elicited from him after a long interrogation. By the time he wrote his name he wasn't sure what he was doing except maybe now they'd let him sleep. His retrial was one of the major New York cases to invoke *Miranda*. And we got him sprung. A little retroactive justice.

"Thank you, man," he said to me, and turned to kiss his tearful wife.

"Stay loose," I answered, moving off, incapable of sharing LeRoy Seeger's happiness. Besides, he had a wife. And anyway, the world was full of what in lawyers' slang we call "screwees."

8

Like Sandy Webber, who was dueling with his draft board to get C.O. status. They were vacillating. Sandy wasn't Quaker, so it wasn't clear that it was "deeply held belief" and not just cowardice that made him want to not make war. Although it looked precarious, he wouldn't go to Canada. He wanted the acknowledgment that he could own his conscience. He was gentle. And his girl was scared as hell for him. One of his friends was doing time in Lewisburg and not enjoying it. Let's split to Montreal, she said. I want to stay and fight, he said.

We did. We lost. Then we appealed and won. He was glad to get three years of washing dishes in a hospital.

"You were just fantastic," Sandy and his lady sang, embracing me together. I answered, "Keep the faith." And started walking off to slay more dragons. I looked back just once and saw them dancing on the sidewalk. And wished that I could smile.

Oh, I was very angry.

I worked as late as possible. I didn't like to leave the office. Everything in our apartment somehow emanated Jenny. The piano. And her books. The furniture we picked together. Yeah, I sort of told myself that I should move. But I got me home so late it didn't seem to matter. Gradually I got accustomed to my solo dinners in our quiet kitchen, playing tapes alone at night—although I never sat in Jenny's reading chair. I had even almost taught myself to get to sleep in our so-empty bed. And so I didn't think I had to leave the place.

Until I opened up a door.

It was Jenny's closet, which I had avoided till that day. But somehow, foolishly, I opened it. And saw her clothing. Jenny's dresses and her blouses and her scarves. Her sweaters—even one from high school she'd refused to toss away and used to wear, as mangy as it was, around the house. All of it was there and Jenny wasn't. I can't tell you what I thought as I stood staring at those silk and woolen souvenirs. Like maybe if I touched that ancient sweater I might feel a molecule of living Jenny.

I closed the door and never opened it again.

Two weeks later Philip Cavilleri quietly packed all her stuff and took it off. He mumbled that he knew this Catholic group that helped the poor. And just before he left for Cranston in his borrowed baker's truck, he said in valediction, "I won't visit you again unless you move."

Funny. Once he had despoiled the house of everything that wakened Jenny in the mind, I found a new apartment in a week. Small and prisonlike (the first-floor windows in New York have iron bars, remember?), it was the not-quite basement of a brownstone where a rich producer lived. His fancy gold-knobbed door was up a flight of steps, so people headed for his orgies never bothered me. Also it was closer to the office and just half a block from Central Park. Obviously, signs were pointing to my imminent recovery.

Still I have a serious confession.

Even though I'm in new quarters all refurnished with new posters and a brand-new bed, and friends more often say, "You're looking good, old buddy," there is something that I've kept of Jenny, who was once my wife.

In the bottom drawer of the desk at home are Jenny's glasses. Yes. Both pairs of Jenny's glasses. Because a glance at them reminds me of the lovely eyes that looked through them to look through me.

But otherwise, as anyone who sees me never hesitates to say, I'm in terrific shape.

3

"Hi, my name is Phil. I'm into baking cookies."

Incredible! The way he'd caught the lingo, you would think that cupcakes were his hobby, not his livelihood.

"Hi there, Phil, I'm Jan. Your friend is cute."

"And so is yours," said Phil, as if to all this bullshit born.

This scintillating repartee was taking place in Maxwell's Prune, a very fancy singles bar at Sixty-fourth and First. Well, actually, its name is Maxwell's Plum, but my pervasive cynicism shrivels up the fruit of everybody else's optimism. Simply put, I hate the joint. I can't abide those self-styled beautiful young swingers chattering euphorically. And coming on like they were millionaires or literary critics. Or even really single.

"This is Oliver," said Philip Cavilleri, suit by Robert Hall, coiffure by Dom of Cranston, cashmere sweater by Cardin (through Filene's basement).

"Hi, Ol," said Jan. "You're very cute. Are you a cookie-lover too?"

She maybe was a model. What the magazines call statuesque. To me she looked like a giraffe. And of course she had a roly-poly friend. Marjory, who giggled when presented.

"Do you come here often?" queried Jan, the statuesque giraffe.

"Never," I replied.

"Yeah, that's what everybody says. I only come on weekends. I'm from out of town."

"What a coincidence," said Phil. "I also hail from out of town."

"And you?" said Jan to me.

"I'm out to lunch," I said.

"No shit," said Jan.

"He means," my colleague Philip interposed, "we'd like to ask you both to dinner."

"Cool," said Jan.

We dined in some place down the block called Flora's Rib Cage.

"Very in," said Jan.

But I might add not very inexpensive. Phil outwrestled me to get the check (although he couldn't hide his shock upon perusing it). He grandiosely paid it with his Master Charge. I imagined he would have to sell enormous quantities of cookies for this gesture. . . .

"Are you very rich?" said giggly Marge to Phil.

"Well, let us say I am a man of means," the Duke of Cranston answered, adding, "though I'm not as cultured as my son-in-law."

There was a little pause. Ah, quite a sticky wicket, this.

"Son-in-law?" said Jan. "You two are, you know . . . ?" And she waved her bony, long-nailed hand in interrogatory circles.

Phil did not know how to answer, so I helped him, nodding yes.

"Hey, wow," said Jan, "that's far-out wild. But where's your wives?"

"Well . . . uh," said Phil, "they're . . ."

Now another pause as Philip groped for equilibrium.

"Not in town," I said, to spare him more embarrassment.

There was another pause as Jan absorbed the scene.

"That's cool," she said.

Phil was looking at the murals on the walls and I was at the limit of my patience.

"Girls," I said, "I gotta leave."

"Why?" asked Jan.

"I have a porno film to go to." And I edged away.

"Hey, *that* is weird," I heard the lissome Jan exclaim. "That creep goes out to porno films alone?"

"Oh, I don't go to them," I called across the crowded room. "I *act* in them."

Seconds later, Phil had reached me on the street.

"Hey, look," he said. "You gotta start."

"Okay, we started."

"So then why'd you leave?"

"The utter joy was killing me," I said.

We walked in silence.

"Look," said Philip finally. "It was a way of getting back to things."

"There's gotta be a better way."

"Like what?"

"Oh, I don't know," I said facetiously. "I'll take an ad."

That shut him up for several seconds. Then he said, "You did already."

"*What?*" I stopped and looked at him, incredulous. "I *what?*"

"You know that fancy book review that Jenny used to read? I took an ad for you. Don't worry. Real discreet. With class. Sophisticated."

"Oh," I said. "Like what exactly was the essence?"

"Well, sort of 'New York lawyer heavy into sports and anthropology—'"

"Where the hell'd you get the anthropology?"

He shrugged. "I thought it sounded intellectual."

"Oh, great. I'm all aglow to read the answers."

"Here," he said. And from his pocket drew three different envelopes.

"What did they say?"

"I don't read other people's mail," said Philip Cavilleri, staunch defender of the right to privacy.

So there, beneath an orange tungsten street lamp, my bemusement tinged with trepidation—not to mention Philip at my shoulder—I laid bare a sample message.

Holy shit! I thought but didn't say. Phil, pretending that he wasn't reading, simply gasped, "My God!"

The correspondent was indeed a person into anthropology. But this epistle was proposing pagan rites so wild and strange that Philip nearly fainted.

"It's a joke," he mumbled feebly.

"Yes. On you," I answered.

"But who could like such weirdness, Oliver?"

"Philip, it's a brave new world," I said, and smiled to camouflage my own astonishment. I tossed the other letters in a bin.

"Hey, I'm sorry," Philip said, after a block or two of very chastened speechlessness. "I really didn't know."

I put my arm around his shoulder and began to laugh. Relieved, he chuckled too.

We wended homeward in the balmy New York evening. Just the two of us. Because our wives were . . . not in town.

It helps to run.

It clears the mind. Releases tension. And it's socially acceptable to do alone. So even when I'm working on some crucial case, or if I've spent all day in court, and even if it's Washington or anywhere, I put my sweat suit on and run.

Once upon a time I did play squash. But that requires certain other skills. Like eloquence enough to say, "Nice shot" or "Do you think we'll mangle Yale this year?" That far transcends my current capabilities. And so I run. Working out in Central Park, I never have to speak to anyone.

"Hey, Oliver, you s.o.b.!"

One afternoon I seemed to hear my name. Just imagination. No one ever paged me in the park. And so I jogged along.

"You goddamn Harvard snob!"

Although the world abounds with guys of that description, still I somehow sensed that I indeed was being called. I looked back and saw my former college roommate, Stephen Simpson, '64, about to overtake me on his bike.

"Hey, what the hell is wrong with you?" he said by way of salutation.

"Simpson, what gives you the right to say that anything is wrong with me?"

"Well, first, I'm now a graduated doctor; second, I'm supposed to be your friend; and third, I leave you messages you never answer."

"I figured med school students never have the time . . ."

"Hey, Barrett, I was busy, but I found the time to marry Gwen. I called—I even telegrammed an invitation to your office—and you didn't show."

"Gee, I'm sorry, Steve, I never got the message," I prevaricated.

"Yeah? How come you sent a wedding present two weeks later?"

Jesus Christ, this Simpson shoulda been a lawyer! But how could I explain that all I really wanted was a leave of absence from the human race?

"I'm sorry, Steve," I answered, hoping he would ride on by.

"You're not sorry, you're pathetic."

"Thanks. Regards to Gwen." He didn't leave my side.

"Hey, look—don't ask me why, but Gwen would love to see you," Simpson said.

"That's awfully masochistic. Has she seen a doctor?"

"Me. I told her she was off her rocker. But since we can't afford the theater, you're the cheapest way to get some laughs. How's Friday night?"

"I'm busy, Simpson."

"Sure, I know. There's always night court. Anyway, show up at eight."

He then accelerated by me, turning back but once. To say, as if addressing one of limited intelligence, "That's eight P.M. this Friday night. We're in the goddamn book, so no excuses."

"Forget it, Steve. I won't be there!"

He pretended not to hear my firm rebuttal. Goddamn arrogance to think I could be pushed around.

Anyway, the guy in Sherry-Lehmann claimed that Château Lynch-Bages, though a mere fifth growth, was very underrated and among the best Bordeaux ("Charming, round and witty"). So I got two bottles ('64). Even if the Simpsons would be bored to tears, they'd have a clever wine for consolation.

They acted pleased to see me.

"Oliver, you haven't changed a bit!"

"You haven't either, Gwen!"

I noticed that they also hadn't changed their posters. Andy Warhol at his Poppiest. ("I saw so damn much Campbell soup when I was young, I'd never hang it on the wall!" my wife remarked when we had visited them years ago.)

We sat down on the floor. From corner speakers Paul and Art were softly asking if we were goin' to Scarborough Fair. Stephen opened some Mondavi white. I munched innumerable pretzels as we talked of metaphysical profundities. Like what a drag it was to be a resident, how rarely she and Steve could have a quiet evening. And of course, did I esteem that Harvard had a chance to mangle Yale that year? Gwen didn't specify what sport. She could have asked if Yin would mangle Yang. But let it pass. The point is that they tried to make me feel that I could loosen up. It wasn't half as bad as I'd imagined.

Then suddenly a bell rang and I froze.

"What's that?" I asked.

"Stay loose," said Steve. "It's just the other guests."

I'd accurately sensed conspiracy in that bell's timbre.

"What other guests?" I asked.

"Well, actually," said Gwen, "it's just a single guest."

"You mean a guest who's single, right?" I said, now feeling like a cornered animal.

"By chance," said Steve, and left to get the door.

Dammit, this is why I *never* go to other people's houses! I can't endure the friends who try to "help." I knew the whole scenario already. This would be a former roommate or an older sister or a classmate who was getting a divorce. Yet another ambush, dammit!

Inwardly enraged, I wanted to say, "Fuck." But since I didn't know Gwen well enough, I just said, "Shit."

"Oliver, it's someone nice."

"I'm sorry, Gwen. I know you both meant well, but—"

At that very moment Steve returned with this night's sacrificial victim.

Wire glasses.

What I noticed first was she was wearing rounded wire glasses. And was taking off her clothes. I mean the jacket she was wearing, which was white.

Simpson introduced Joanna Stein, M.D., a resident in pediatrics, whom he'd gone to med school with. They currently were slaving in the selfsame hospital. I didn't even pay enough attention to decide if she was pretty. Someone said let's all sit down and have a drink and so we did.

Lots of small talk after that.

Gradually I noticed that Joanna Stein, M.D., besides her rounded wire glasses, had a gentle voice. Later still I noticed that the thoughts articulated in that voice were sensitive and kind. I'm glad to say there was no mention of my "case." I guess the Simpsons briefed her.

"It's a crappy life," I heard Steve Simpson say.

"I'll drink to that," I said. And then I realized he and Gwen were just commiserating with Joanna on how hard it was to be a resident.

"What do you do for recreation, Jo?" said I. And wondered, Christ, I hope she doesn't think I'm hinting that I want to ask her out.

"I go to bed," she answered.

"Oh?"

"I can't help it," she continued. "I get home so tired I just crash and sleep for twenty hours."

"Oh."

There was a pause. Who now would take the ball of conversation and attempt to pass or run for yardage? We sat in silence for what seemed a century. Until Gwen Simpson bade us come to dinner.

May I say in total candor that although Gwen is a lovely human being, she is not exactly gifted in the culinary arts. Sometimes when she simply boils up water it can taste all *burned*. Tonight was no exception. One could even claim she'd . . . overdone herself. But still I ate, in order not to have to talk. At least there were two doctors present should my stomach later need emergency attention.

And as things wore on, as we were savoring—would you believe—a cheesecake that seemed charcoal broiled, Joanna Stein inquired, "Oliver?"

Thanks to my experience in cross-examination, I responded quickly.

"Yes?"

"Do you like opera?"

Dammit, that's a tricky question, I thought inwardly, while racing to consider what she might intend. Would she want to speak of operas like *Bohème* or *Traviata*, works in which, by chance, a lady dies in the finale? Just to offer me catharsis, maybe? No, she couldn't be that gauche. But anyway, the room was hushed awaiting my reply.

"Oh, I don't mind opera," I replied, then shrewdly covering all bases, added, "I just don't dig anything Italian, French or German."

"Good," she said, unfazed. Could she have meant the Chinese opera?

"Merritt's singing Purcell Tuesday night."

Dammit, I forgot to rule out English too! Now I'd probably got involved in taking her to some damn Limey opera.

"Sheila Merritt's this year's big soprano," Stephen Simpson said, now double-teaming me.

"And she's singing *Dido and Aeneas*," added Gwen, thus making it a three-on-one encounter. (Dido—yet another girl who dies because the guy she went with was a selfish bastard!)

"That sounds great," I said, capitulating. Though inwardly I cursed both Steve and Gwen. And most of all, Château Lynch-Bages, for weakening my first intention, which was to say that any music made me sick.

"Oh, I'm pleased," Joanna said. "I've got two seats . . ."

Ah, here it comes.

". . . but Steve and I are both on duty. I was hoping you and Gwen could use the tickets."

"Gwen would really dig it, Oliver," said Steve, his tone of voice implying that his wife deserved a break.

"Yeah, fine," I said. Then realizing I should act a little more enthused, I told Joanna, "Thanks a lot."

"I'm glad that you can go," she said. "Please tell my parents that you saw me and I'm still alive."

What was this? I now cringed inwardly, while picturing a seat adjoining the aggressive ("Like my daughter?") mother of Joanna Stein.

"They're in the strings," she said, and hurried out with Steve.

Sitting there with Gwen, I thought of punishing myself for my absurd behavior. So I tried to chew another piece of charcoal cheesecake.

"Where the hell is 'Strings'?" I asked her.

"Usually it's eastward of the woodwinds. Joanna's mother's a violist and her father plays the cello with the New York City Opera."

"Oh," I said, and took a mouthful more of punishment.

A pause.

"Was it really all that painful meeting Jo?" she asked.

I looked at her.

And answered, "Yeah."

When I am laid . . .

Thus begins the song that was the hit of 1689. The problem with an English opera is that sometimes you can understand the words.

When I am laid—
Am laid in earth
May my wrongs create no trouble—
No trouble in thy breast . . .

Dido, queen of Carthage, was about to self-destruct and felt the need to tell the world about it in an aria. The music was fantastic and the text antique. Sheila Merritt sang it brilliantly and well deserved all her ovations. Finally she died definitively, dancing Cupids scattered roses, and the curtain fell.

"Hey, Gwen, I'm glad I came," I said, as we arose.

"Let's thank our benefactors," she replied.

We threaded through the people moving out and reached the orchestra.

"Where's Steve?" said Mr. Stein as he was covering his cello. He had flowing grayish hair that didn't seem acquainted with a comb.

"He's on duty with Joanna," Gwen replied. "This is Oliver, a friend of hers." (She didn't have to put it quite that way!) At this moment, bearing her viola, Mrs. Stein approached. Sort of small and stocky, though her effervescent manner made her quite attractive.

"Are you holding court, King Stein?"

"As usual, my dear," he answered, adding, "Gwen you've met. And this is Oliver, a friend of Jo's."

"Nice to meet you. How's our daughter?"

"Fine," retorted Mr. Stein, before I could respond.

"I didn't ask you, did I, Stein?" said Mrs. Stein.

"Jo is fine," I said, not quite in sync with all their badinage. "And thank you for the seats."

"Did you enjoy it?" Mrs. Stein inquired.

"Of course. It was terrific!" said her husband.

"Who asked *you?*" said Mrs. Stein.

"I'm answering for him because I'm a professional. And I can tell you Merritt was superb."

Then back to me, "Old Purcell could write music, huh? That finale—all those great chromatic changes in the downward tetrachord!"

"Perhaps he didn't notice, Stein," said Mrs. Stein.

"He *had* to. Merritt sang the thing four times!"

"Excuse him, Oliver," said Mrs. Stein to me. "He's only crazy when it comes to music."

"What else is there?" Stein retorted, adding, "Everyone's invited Sunday. Our place. Half past five. That's when we'll really play."

"We can't," said Gwen, at last returning to the conversation. "It's Stephen's parents' anniversary."

"Okay," said Mr. Stein. "Then Oliver—"

"He may have other plans," said Mrs. Stein to help me off the hook.

"Who are you to talk for him?" said Stein to Mrs. Stein with righteous indignation. And then to me, "Show up around five-thirty. Bring your instrument."

"The only thing I play is hockey," I replied, in hope that I would gross him out.

"Then bring your stick," said Mr. Stein. "We'll put you by the ice cubes. See you Sunday, Oliver."

"How'd it go?" said Steve, when I deposited his wife.

"Wonderful," Gwen rhapsodized. "You missed a great performance."

"What did Barrett think?" he asked, though I was standing there. I wanted to refer him to my newfound spokesman, Mr. Stein, but simply mumbled, "It was good."

"That's good," said Steve.

But inwardly I paraphrased the late Queen Dido as I thought, Now I am screwed.

Sunday came. And naturally, I didn't want to go. But fate did not come through for me. I didn't get an urgent message on an urgent case. I didn't get a call from Phil. I didn't even get the flu. Thus, lacking an excuse—and carrying a large bouquet—I found myself on Riverside and Ninety-fourth. Outside the door of Louis Stein.

"Aha," sang out the host when he espied my floral offering.

"You shouldn't have." And then called out to Mrs. Stein, "It's Oliver—he brought me flowers!"

She came trotting up and kissed me on the cheek.

"Come in and meet the music *mafiosi*," Mr. Stein commanded. And he put his arm around my shoulder.

Ten or twelve musicians were installed at music stands around the room. Chattering and tuning up. Tuning up and chattering. The mood was upbeat and the volume loud. The only fancy piece of furniture was a large and brightly polished black piano. Through a massive window I could see the Hudson River and the Palisades.

I shook everybody's hand. Most were sort of grown-up hippies. Except the younger ones, who looked like younger hippies. Why the hell had I put on a tie?

"Where's Jo?" I asked to be polite.

"She's on till eight," said Mr. Stein, "but meet her brothers. Marty plays the horn and David winds and flute. You notice they rebelled against their parents. Jo's the only one who even touched a string."

Both were tall and shy. But brother David was so timid he just waved his clarinet in greeting. Marty shook my hand. "Welcome to the music zoo," he said.

"I don't know anything about it, Marty," I confessed uneasily. "Say 'pizzicato' and I'd tell you that it's veal with cheese."

"It is, it is," said Mr. Stein. "And stop apologizing. You're not the first who only came to listen."

"No?" I asked.

"Of course not. My late father couldn't read a note."

"Oliver, please tell him that we're waiting," Mrs. Stein called out, "or else you come and play the cello."

"Patience, darling," said the host. "I'm making sure he feels at home."

"I feel at home," I said obligingly. He stuffed me in a floppy chair, then hurried back to join the orchestra.

It was fascinating. I just sat there watching what my preppie buddies might describe as weirdos making lovely music. Now a

Mozart, now Vivaldi, then a guy called Lully I had never heard of.

After Lully came a Monteverdi and the best pastrami I had ever tasted. In the food break, tall, shy brother David whispered to me in clandestine tones.

"Is it true that you're a hockey player?"

"Was," I said.

"Then can I ask you something?"

"Sure."

"How did the Rangers do today?"

"Gee, I forgot," I said, and clearly disappointed him. How could I explain that Oliver the former hockey maniac was so immersed in legal research he forgot to watch the Rangers beat or lose to his once daily worshipped punching Boston Bruins?

Then Joanna came and kissed me. Actually, it must have been a ritual. She kissed everybody.

"Have they driven you insane?"

"No," I said. "I'm really having fun."

And suddenly it struck me that I wasn't even lying. The harmony I had enjoyed that evening wasn't just the music. It was everywhere. The way they talked. The way they complimented one another on the execution of a tricky passage. All I'd ever known remotely like this was when Harvard hockey jocks would psych each other up to go and trample people.

Only here they were psyched up just playing music side by side. Everywhere I sensed so goddamn much . . . affection.

I had never visited a world like this.

Except with Jenny.

"Get your fiddle, Jo," said Mr. Stein.

"Are you crazy?" she retorted. "I'm so out of shape—"

"You practice medicine too much," he said. "You should be giving music equal time. Besides, I've saved the Bach especially for you."

"No," Joanna answered firmly.

"Come on. Oliver's been waiting just to hear you." Now she blushed. I tried to signal, but to no avail.

Mr. Stein then turned to me. "Tell your friend my daughter to tune up her violin." Before I could react, Joanna, now a maraschino, ceased protesting.

"Okay, Daddy, have it your way. But it won't sound good."

"It will, it will," he answered. Then as she went off, he turned to me again. "You like the Brandenburgs?"

Inwardly I tightened. For these Bach concertos were among the few I did know. Had I not proposed to Jenny after she had played the Fifth and we were walking by the river back at Harvard? Had that music not been something of a prelude to our marriage? The very thought of hearing it began an ache.

"Well?" asked Mr. Stein. Then I realized I had not responded to his friendly query.

"Yes," I said, "I like the Brandenburgs. Which one are you doing?"

"All! Why should we show a favorite?"

"I'm just playing *one*," his daughter called, affecting pique. She now was seated with the violins, engaged in dialogue with some old gentleman who shared her stand. The group was tuning up again. But as the intermission had been laced with booze, the volume was a good deal higher than before.

Mr. Stein had now decided to conduct. "What has Lenny Bernstein got on me? A better hairdo!" He tapped his podium, a TV set.

"Now," he said, his accent suddenly Germanic, "I vant sharp attack. You hear me? *Sharp*."

The orchestra was poised. He raised his pencil for the downbeat.

I held my breath and hoped I would survive.

Then suddenly the guns went off.

I mean a kind of fist artillery upon the door. Too loud and—if I may so judge—quite out of rhythm.

"Open up!" a semihuman voice bellowed.

"Police?" I asked of Jo, who suddenly was at my side.

"They're never in the neighborhood." She smiled. "It's much

too dangerous. No, it's Godzilla from upstairs. His real name's Temple and he's anti-life."

"Open up!!"

I looked around. There were some twenty of us, yet the orchestra seemed cowed. This guy Godzilla must be pretty dangerous. Anyway, Lou Stein unbolted.

"Goddamn hell, you s.o.b.s, I tell you every freakin' Sunday—cut the noise!"

This he said while looming over Mr. Stein. "Godzilla" was indeed quite apt. He was a huge and hairy creature.

"But, Mr. Temple," Mr. Stein replied, "we always end our Sunday sessions right at ten."

"Shit!" the monster snorted.

"Yes, I noticed you had left that out," said Mr. Stein.

Temple glared at him. "Don't push me, creep. I've reached the boilin' point with you!" Hatred smoldered in Godzilla's tones. I sensed his goal in life was to aggress his neighbor Mr. Stein. And now he was about to make a dream come true.

Stein's two sons, though clearly frightened, moved to join their father.

Temple ranted on. And now, with Mrs. Stein already by her husband's side, Joanna slipped away from me and headed for the door. (To fight? To bind the wounds?) It all was happening so fast. And coming to a head.

"Goddammit, don't you lousy bastards know that it's against the law disturbin' other people's peace."

"Excuse me, Mr. Temple, I think you're the one who's violating people's rights."

I just spoke those words! Before I even realized I was going to pronounce them. And, what surprised me more, I had risen and begun approaching the unwanted visitor. Who now turned to me.

"What's your problem, blondie?" said the animal.

I noticed he was several inches taller and had forty pounds (at least) on me. But hopefully not all of it was muscle.

I motioned to the Steins to let me handle this. But they remained.

"Mr. Temple," I continued, "have you ever heard of section forty of the Criminal Code? That's trespassing. Or section seventeen—that's threatening bodily harm? Or section—"

"Whatta you—a cop?" he grunted. Clearly he had known a few.

"Just a lawyer," I replied, "but I could send you up the river for a lengthy rest."

"You're bluffin'," Temple said.

"No. But if you're anxious to resolve this issue sooner, there's another process."

"Yeah, you fruit?"

He flexed his looming muscles. Behind me I could sense the orchestra's anxiety. And inside, a scintilla of my own. But still I calmly took my jacket off, and spoke sotto voce with extreme politeness.

"Mr. Temple, if you don't evaporate, I'll simply have to slowly —as one intellectual to another—beat your Silly Putty brains out."

After the intruder's quite precipitous departure, Mr. Stein broke out champagne ("imported straight from California"). The orchestra then voted to perform the *loudest* piece they knew, a very spirited rendition of Tchaikovsky's 1812 Overture. In which *I* even played an instrument: the cannon (empty ash can).

Several hours later—all too soon—the party ended.

"Come again," said Mrs. Stein.

"Of course he will," said Mr. Stein.

"What makes you so sure?" she asked.

"He loves us," Louis Stein replied.

And that was that.

No one had to tell me that my duty was to take Joanna home. Although the hour was late, she still insisted that we take the number-five bus that goes down Riverside and ultimately snakes across to Fifth. She was sort of tired from her hours of work. And yet her mood was up.

"God, you were fantastic, Oliver," she said. And put her hand on mine.

I tried to ask myself just what I felt about her touch.

And couldn't get an answer.

Joanna still was bubbly.

"Temple won't dare show his mug again!" she said.

"Hey, listen, Jo—it doesn't take much brains to call a bully's bluff."

I'd used my hands to gesture and they now were disengaged from hers. (Relief?)

"But still . . ."

She didn't finish. Maybe it began to puzzle her the way I kept insisting I was just a stupid jock. My only purpose was to let her know I wasn't really worth her time. I mean she was so nice. And kind of pretty. Well, at least a normal guy with normal feelings would have found her so.

She had a fourth-floor walk-up near the hospital. As we stood outside her door, I noticed she was shorter than she'd seemed at first. I mean she had to look straight up at me to talk.

I also noticed that my breath was kind of short. It couldn't be from climbing stairs (I run a lot, remember). And I began to feel the vaguest sense of panic as I talked to this intelligent and gentle doctor lady.

Maybe she'd imagine that I liked her more than just platonically. What if maybe—

"Oliver," Joanna said, "I'd like to ask you in. But I go on at six A.M."

"Another time," I said. And suddenly could feel more oxygen within my lungs.

"I hope so, Oliver."

She kissed me. On the cheek. (They were a bunch of *touchers*, her whole family.)

"Good night," she said.

"I'll call you," I replied.
"I had a lovely evening."
"I did too."

And yet I was ineffably unhappy.

Walking back that night, I came to the conclusion that I needed a psychiatrist.

"Let's begin by leaving out King Oedipus completely."

Thus began my well-prepared self-introduction to the doctor. Finding a reliable psychiatrist involves a simple set of moves. First you call up friends who are physicians and you tell them that a friend of *yours* could use some help. Then they recommend a doctor for this troubled person. Finally, you walk around the phone two hundred times, you dial, and make your first appointment.

"Look," I rambled on, "I've had the courses and I know the jargon we could toss around. How we could label my behavior with my father when I married Jenny. I mean all the things that Freud would say is not the stuff I want to hear."

Dr. Edwin London, though "extremely fine," according to the guy who recommended him, was not, however, too inclined to lengthy sentences.

"Why are you here?" he asked without expression.

Then I got scared. My opening remarks had gone okay, but here we were already in the cross-examination.

Why exactly was I there? What *did* I want to hear? I swallowed and replied so softly that the words were barely audible to me.

"Why I can't feel."

He waited silently.

"Since Jenny died, I just can't feel a thing. Yeah, now and then a twinge of hunger. TV dinners take quick care of that. But otherwise . . . for eighteen months . . . I have felt absolutely nothing."

He listened as I struggled to dredge up my thoughts. They poured out helter-skelter in a stream of hurt. I feel so terrible. Correction, I feel nothing. Which is worse. I'm lost without her. Philip helps. No, Phil can't really help. Although he tries. Feel nothing. Almost two whole years. I can't respond to normal human beings.

Now silence. I was sweating.

"Sexual desire?" asked the doctor.

"None," I said. And then to make it even clearer, "Absolutely nothing."

No immediate reply. Was London shocked? I couldn't read his face. So then, because it was so obvious to both of us, I said:

"No one has to tell me that it's guilt."

Then Dr. Edwin London spoke his longest sentence of the day.

"Do you feel . . . responsible for Jenny's death?"

Did I feel responsible for Jenny's death? I thought immediately of my compulsive wish to die the day that Jenny did. But that was transient. I know I didn't give my wife leukemia. And yet . . .

"Maybe. For a while I guess I did. But basically my anger was against myself. For all the things I should have done while she was still alive."

There was a pause and Dr. London said, "Such as?"

I talked again of my estrangement from my family. How I had

let the circumstances of my marriage to a girl of slightly (hugely!) different social background be a declaration of my independence. Watch, Big Daddy Rich-with-Bucks, I'll make it on my goddamn own.

Except one thing. I made it rough on Jenny. Not just emotionally. Though that was bad enough, considering her passion when it came to honoring your parents. But even worse was my refusal to take anything from them. To me this was a source of pride. But shit, to Jenny, who'd grown up in poverty, what could be new and wonderful about not having money in the bank?

"And just to serve my arrogance, she had to make so many sacrifices."

"Do you think she thought of them as sacrifices?" asked London, probably intuiting that Jenny never once complained.

"Doctor, what she may have thought no longer is the point." He looked at me.

For half a second I was frightened I might . . . cry.

"Jenny's dead and only now I see how selfishly I acted." There was a pause.

"How?" he asked.

"We were graduating. Jenny had this scholarship to France. When we decided to get married there was never any question. We just *knew* we'd stay in Cambridge and I'd go to law school. *Why?*"

There was another silence. Dr. London did not speak. So I continued ranting.

"Why the hell did that appear the only logical alternative? My goddamn arrogance! To just assume *my* life was more important!"

"There were things you couldn't know," said Dr. London. It was a gauche attempt to mollify my guilt.

"Still I knew—goddammit—that she'd never been to Europe! Couldn't I have gone with her and been a lawyer one year later?"

Maybe he might think this was some ex post facto guilt from reading women's lib material. It wasn't that. I didn't hurt so much from stopping Jenny's "higher studies," but for keeping her from tasting Paris. Seeing London. Feeling Italy.

"Do you understand?" I asked.

There was another pause.

"Are you prepared to spend some time on this?" he asked.

"That's why I came."

"Tomorrow, five o'clock?"

I nodded. And he nodded. I left.

I walked along Park Avenue to get myself together. And to gear myself for what would lie ahead. Tomorrow we would start the surgery. Incisions in the soul I knew would hurt. I was prepared for that.

I only wondered what the hell I'd find.

It took about a week to get to Oedipus.

Who has a palace on the Harvard campus: Barrett Hall.

"My family donated it to buy respectability."

"Why?" Dr. London asked.

"Because our money isn't clean. Because my ancestors were pioneers in sweatshop labor. Our philanthropy is just a recent hobby."

Curious to say, I learned this not from any book about the Barretts, but . . . at Harvard.

When I was a college senior, I needed distribution credits. Hence along with hordes of others I took Soc. Sci. 108, American Industrial Development. The teacher was a so-called radical economist named Donald Vogel. He had already earned a place in Harvard history by interweaving all his data with obscenities. Furthermore, his course was famed because it was a total gut.

("I don't believe in *blanking blanking blank* examinations," Vogel said. The masses cheered.)

It would be an understatement to report the hall was packed. It overflowed with lazy jocks and zealous pre-med students, all in quest of lack of work.

Usually, despite Don Vogel's indigo vocabulary, most of us would get some extra *zzz's* or read the *Crimson*. Then one day, unfortunately, I tuned in. The subject was the early U.S. textile industry, a likely soporific.

"*Blank*, when it comes to textiles, many *blanking* 'noble' Harvard names played very sordid roles. Take, for instance, Amos Brewster Barrett, Harvard class of 1794. . . ."

Holy shit—*my family!* Did Vogel know that I was out there listening? Or did he give this lecture to his mob of students every year?

I scrunched down in my seat as he continued.

"In 1814, Amos and some other Harvard cronies joined forces to bring the industrial revolution to Fall River, Massachusetts. They built the first big textile factories. And 'took care' of all their workers. It's called paternalism. For morals' sake, they housed the girls recruited from the distant farms in dormitories. Of course the company deducted half their meager pay for food and lodging.

"The little ladies worked an eighty-hour week. And naturally the Barretts taught them to be frugal. 'Put your money in the bank, girls.' Guess who also owned the banks?"

I longed to metamorphose into a mosquito, just to buzz away.

Orchestrated by an even more than usual cascade of epithets, Don Vogel chronicled the growth of Barrett enterprise. He continued for the better (or the worse) part of an hour.

In the early nineteenth century, half the workers in Fall River were mere children. Some as young as *five*. The kids took home two bucks a week, the women three, the men a princely seven and a half.

But not all cash, of course. Part was paid to them in coupons. Valid only in the Barrett stores. Of course.

Vogel gave examples of how bad conditions were. For instance, in the weaving room, humidity improves the quality of cloth. So owners would *inject* more steam into their plants. And in the peak of summer, windows were kept closed to keep the warp and filling damp. This did not endear the Barretts to the workers.

"And dig this *blanking blanking* fact," Don Vogel fumed. "It wasn't bad enough with all the squalor and the filth—or all those accidents not covered by the slightest compensation—but their *blanking* pay went *down!* The Barrett profits soared and yet they *cut* the *blanking* workers' pay! 'Cause each new wave of immigrants would work for even less!

"Blank blank blanking blanking blank!"

Later that semester I was grinding in the Radcliffe Library. There I met a girl. Jenny Cavilleri, '64. Her father was a pastry chef from Cranston. Her late mother, T'resa Verna Cavilleri, was the daughter of Sicilians who had emigrated to . . . Fall River, Massachusetts.

"Now can you understand why I resent my family?"

There was a pause.

"Five o'clock tomorrow," Dr. London said.

I ran.

When I left the doctor's office I felt much more angry and confused than when I had begun. And thus the only therapy for therapy seemed to be running hard in Central Park. Since our chance reunion I had managed to con Simpson into working out with me. So whenever hospital commitments gave him time, we'd meet and circumambulate the reservoir.

Happily, he never asked me if I ever followed up with Miss Joanna Stein. Did she ever tell him? Had she diagnosed me too? Anyway, the subject was conspicuously absent from our dialogues. Frankly, I think Steve was satisfied that I was talking to humanity again. I never bullshit with my friends and so I told him I had started seeing a psychiatrist. I didn't offer details and he didn't ask.

This afternoon, my session with the doctor had me very agitated and unwittingly I ran too fast for Steve. After just a single lap, he had to stop.

"Hey, man, you go this one alone," he puffed. "I'll pick you up on number three."

I was pretty tired too, and so I slowly jogged to get my own breath back. Nonetheless, I trotted by some of the many athletes who appear at eventide in multicolored, multiformed and multipaced variety. Of course the New York club guys would go by me like a shot. And all the high school studs could dust me off.

But even when I jogged I did my share of passing: senior citizens, fat ladies and most children under twelve.

Now I was flagging and my vision slightly blurred. Sweat got in my eyes and all I vaguely could perceive of those I passed was shape and size and color of their plumage. Hence I can't accurately say just who was running to and fro. Until the incident I now relate.

A form was visible some eighty yards ahead of me, the sweatsuit blue Adidas (i.e., quite expensive) and the pace respectable. I'll groove along and gradually pick off this . . . girl? Or else a slender boy with long blond hair.

I didn't gain, so I accelerated toward the blue Adidas. It took twenty seconds to get close. Indeed, it was a girl. Or else a guy with a fantastic ass—and I would have another issue to discuss with Dr. London. But no, as I drew nearer still, I definitely saw a slender lady whose blond tresses were a-blowing in the wind. Okay, Barrett, make like you're Bob Hayes and pass this runner with panache. I revved up, shifted gears and gracefully gunned by. Now on to newer challenges. Up ahead I recognized that burly opera singer whom I regularly took in stride. Mr. Baritone, you're Oliver's next victim.

Then a figure passed me in a flash of blue. It had to be a sprinter from the Millrose Club. But no. The azure form was that same nylon-packaged female whom I'd calculated to be twenty yards behind me. But now she was ahead again. Perhaps it was some new phenom I should have read about. I shifted gears again to get another look. It wasn't easy. I was tired, she was going pretty well. I caught up at last. Her front was even nicer than her back.

"Hey—are you some champion?" I inquired.

"Why do you ask?" she said, not very out of breath.

"You went right by me like a shot. . . ."

"You weren't going all that fast," she answered.

Hey, was that supposed to be an insult? Who the hell was she?

"Hey, was that supposed to be an insult?"

"Only if you've got a fragile ego," she replied.

Although my confidence is shatterproof, I nonetheless was pissed.

"You're pretty cocky," I replied.

"Was *that* supposed to be an insult?" she inquired.

"It was," I said. Not masking it, as she did.

"Would you rather run alone?" she asked.

"I would," I said.

"Okay," she said. And sprinted suddenly ahead. Now she was smoking—obviously just a ploy—but I was damned if I'd be bluffed. Acceleration now took total effort. But I caught her.

"Hi."

"I thought you wanted solitude," she said.

Breath was short and hence the dialogue was likewise.

"What team do you run for?"

"None," she said. "I only run to help my tennis."

"Ah, the total jock," I said, deliberately to slight her femininity.

"Yes," she said demurely. "And yourself, are you the total prick?"

How to deal with this, especially when straining to keep running at her pace?

"Yes," I managed. Which in retrospect was just about the wisest thing I could have said. "How's your tennis, anyway?"

"You wouldn't want to play me."

"Yes I would."

"You would?" she said. And slowed—thank God—to walk.

"Tomorrow?"

"Sure," I puffed.

"At six? The Gotham Tennis Club on Ninety-fourth and First."

"I work till six," I said. "How's seven?"

"No, I meant the morning," she replied.

"Six A.M.? Who plays at six A.M.?" I said.

"We do—unless you chicken out," she answered.

"Oh, not at all," I said, regaining breath and wit near simultaneously.

She smiled at that. She had a lot of teeth.

"That's fine. The court's reserved for Marcie Nash—who, by the way, is me."

And then she offered me her hand. To shake, not to kiss, of course. Unlike what I had readied for, she didn't have a jocklike, crushing grip. It was normal. Even delicate.

"And may I know your name?" she said.

I thought I'd be a trifle jocular.

"Gonzales, madam. Pancho B. Gonzales."

"Oh," she said, "I knew it wasn't Speedy Gonzales."

"No," I said, surprised she'd heard about the legendary Speedy, the protagonist of many filthy jokes in many filthy locker rooms.

"Okay, Pancho, six A.M. But don't forget to bring your ass."

"Why?" I queried.

"Naturally," she said, "so I can whip it."

I could counter that.

"Of course. And naturally, you'll bring the balls?"

"Of course," she said. "A lady in New York is lost without them."

With that she ran off at a sprint that Jesse Owens would have envied.

At 5 A.M. New York is dark both physically and metaphorically. From down the block, its second floor illuminated, the tennis club seemed like a baby's night light for the sleeping city. I entered, signed the register, and was directed to the locker rooms. Yawning constantly, I changed and strolled out to the playing area. Lights from all those tennis courts near blinded me. And every one was in full use. These go-go Gothamites about to start their frantic day all seemed to need a frantic tennis session to prepare them for the Game Out There.

Anticipating that Miss Marcie Nash would wear the chicest tennis togs available, I clad myself as shabbily as possible. My uniform was what the fashion page might call "off white." In truth, it was the end result of accidentally mixing many colored garments in the laundromat. Further, I selected what I called my Stan Kowalski shirt. Although it actually was grungier than anything that Marlon Brando ever wore. I was sartorially subtle. Or in other words, a slob.

And just as I expected, she had neon balls. The yellow and fluorescent kind the pros all use.

"Good morning, Merry Sunshine."

She was there already, practicing her serves into the net.

"Hey, you know it's absolutely dark outside?" I said.

"That's precisely why we're playing *inside*, Sancho."

"Pancho," I corrected her, "Miss Narcie Mash . . ."

For I could josh with nomenclature too.

"Sticks and stones may break my bones, but nothing ever breaks my serve," she said, still slamming. Marcie's hair, which on the track had floated in the breeze, was now tied back into a horse's tail. (I'd have to make a pun on that.) And, typical pretentious tennis player, she had sweatbands on both wrists.

"Call me what you wish, dear Pancho. Can we start to play?"

"What for?" I asked.

"I beg your pardon?" Marcie said.

"The stakes," I said. "What are we playing for?"

"Oh, isn't fun enough?" said Marcie Nash demurely and ingenuously.

"Nothing's fun at six A.M.," I said. "I need a tangible incentive."

"Half a buck," she said.

"Was that a reference to my personality?" I asked.

"Hey, you're a wit. No, I meant fifty cents."

"Uhn-uhn." I shook my head and indicated that it had to be substantial. If she played at Gotham she could not be impecunious. Unless she'd joined on spec. That is, in hope the bread she'd cast on membership would soon return as wedding cake.

"Are you rich?" she said to me.

"How is that relevant?" I answered, ever on the defense, since the fates have forced me to be linked to Barrett money bags.

"Just to know how much you can afford to lose," she said.

Tricky question, that. My problem was to find out how much *she* could part with. And so I figured something that would save our mutually smirking faces.

"Look," I said, "why don't we say the loser takes the winner out to dinner. And the winner picks the place."

"I pick '21,'" she said.

"A trifle prematurely," I remarked. "But since I'll take it too, please be forewarned: I eat as much as any elephant."

"I have no doubt," she said. "You run like one."

This psyching had to stop. Goddammit, let's begin!

I played with her. I mean I wanted to humiliate her in the end and thus I played the bluffer's game. I missed some easy shots.

Reacted slowly. Never charged up to the net. Meanwhile Marcie bit, and played all out.

Actually, she wasn't bad. Her moves were swift. Her shots were almost always accurately placed. Her serve was strong and had some spin. Yeah, she had practiced often and was fairly good.

"Hey, you're not too bad at all."

Thus Marcie Nash to *me,* after lengthy although indecisive play. We had traded games about as evenly as I could manage. With my lethal shots still deep inside my hustler's closet. And in fact, I'd let her break my "Simple Simon" service several times.

"I'm afraid we'll have to knock off soon," she said. "I have to be at work by half past eight."

"Gee whiz," I said (how's that for masking my aggression?), "can't we play just one last game? I mean for fun? We'll call it sudden death and winner gets the dinner."

"Well, okay," Marcie Nash conceded, seeming nonetheless a trifle worried that she might be late. Dear me. The boss might be annoyed and not promote her. Yea, ambition should be made of sterner stuff.

"Just one quick game," she said, reluctantly.

"Miss Nash," I said, "I promise you this game will be the swiftest of your life."

And so it was. I let her serve. But now, not only did I charge the net—I virtually stampeded it. Whambam, thank you, ma'am. Marcie Nash was literally shell-shocked. And she never scored a point.

"Holy shit," she said, "you hustled me!"

"Let's say I took a while in warming up," I answered. "Gee whiz, I hope this doesn't make you late for work."

"That's okay—I mean, that's fine," she stammered, somewhat traumatized. "Eight o'clock at '21'?"

I nodded yeah. "Shall I book it for 'Gonzales'?" she inquired.

"No, that's just my racket name. Otherwise they call me Barrett. Oliver 'The Great Pretender' Barrett."

"Oh," she said. "I like Gonzales better." And then sprinted to the ladies' locker room. For some strange reason, I began to smile.

"What amuses you?"

"I beg your pardon?"

"You're smiling," Dr. London said.

"It's a long and boring story," I insisted. Yet I nonetheless explained what seemed to make morose, depressive Barrett doff his tragic mask.

"It's not the girl herself," I told him in summation, "it's the principle. I love to put aggressive women down."

"And there's nothing else?" inquired the doctor.

"Nothing," I replied. "She's even got a mediocre backhand."

She was dressed in money.

I don't mean the slightest bit flamboyant. Quite the opposite. She radiated the supreme in ostentation—absolute simplicity. Her hairdo seemed free-flowing and yet flawless. As if a chic photographer had caught it with a high-speed lens.

This was disconcerting. The utter neatness of Miss Marcie Nash, her perfect posture, her composure, made me feel like last week's spinach scrunched haphazardly into a Baggie. Clearly she must be a model. Or at least do something in the fashion game.

I reached her table. It was in a quiet corner.

"Hi," she said.

"I hope I didn't keep you waiting."

"Actually, you're early," she replied.

"That must mean that you came even earlier," I said.

"I'd say that was a logical conclusion, Mr. Barrett." She smiled. "Are you going to sit down or are you waiting for permission?"

I sat down.

"What are you drinking?" I inquired, pointing at the orange-colored liquid in her glass.

"Orange juice," she said.

"And what?"

"And ice."

"That's all?"

She nodded yes. Before I could ask why she was abstemious, a waiter was at hand, and welcomed us as if we ate there every day.

"And how are we tonight?"

"We're fine. What's good?" I said, unable to sustain this kind of phony badinage.

"The scallops are superb. . . ."

"A Boston specialty," I said, a sudden gastronomic chauvinist.

"Ours are from Long Island," he replied.

"Okay, we'll see how they stand up." I turned to Marcie. "Shall we try the local imitation?"

Marcie smiled assent.

"And to begin?" The waiter looked at her.

"Hearts of lettuce with a drop of lemon juice."

Now I knew for sure she was a model. Otherwise the self-starvation made no sense. Meanwhile I requested fettucini ("Don't be stingy with the butter"). Our host then bowed and scraped away.

We were alone.

"Well, here we are," I said. (And I confess I had rehearsed this opening all afternoon.)

Before she could concur that we indeed were there, a new arrival greeted us.

"The wine, m'sieu?"

I queried Marcie.

"Get something just for you," she said.

"Not even wine?"

"I'm very chaste in that respect," she said, "but I would recommend a nice Meursault for you. Your victory would otherwise be incomplete."

"Meursault," I told the sommelier.

"A 'sixty-six, if possible," said Marcie just to help. He evaporated and we were alone again.

"Why don't you drink at all?" I asked.

"No principles involved. I simply like to keep control of all my senses."

What the hell was that supposed to mean? What senses did she have in mind?

"So you're from Boston?" Marcie said (our dialogue was not exactly loose).

"I am," I said. "And you?"

"I'm not from Boston," she replied.

Was that a subtle put-down?

"Are you in the fashion business?" I inquired.

"Partially. And you?"

"I'm into liberties," I answered.

"Taking them or giving them?" Her smile distracted me from telling if she'd been sarcastic.

"I try to make the government behave," I said.

"That isn't easy," Marcie said.

"Well, I haven't quite succeeded yet."

The sommelier arrived and ceremoniously filled my glass. Then I myself began a vintage flow. What you might call a magnum of description. On what progressive lawyers were involved in at this point in time.

I do confess I didn't know quite how to talk to . . . girls.

I mean it had been many years since I'd been on what you might call a date. I sensed that tales of self would not be cool. ("That egomaniac!" she'd tell her roommate.)

Hence we discussed—or rather I discoursed upon—the Warren Court's decisions on the rights of individuals. And would the Burger kings continue to enhance the Fourth Amendment? That depends on who they choose to fill the Fortas seat. Keep your copy of the Constitution, Marcie, it may soon be out of print!

As I was moving to the First Amendment, waiters swooped upon us with Long Island scallops. Yeah, they aren't bad. But not as good as Boston. Anyway, about the First—the high court rulings are ambiguous! How can they in *O'Brien* v. *U.S.* say that it's *not* symbolic speech to burn a draft card and turn right around in *Tinker* v. *Des Moines* and rule that wearing armbands to protest the war is "purest speech." What the hell, I ask you, is their real position?

"Don't *you* know?" asked Marcie. And before I could assess if she was subtly implying that I'd spoken far too much, the maître d' was present once again to ask what we would like "to top it off." I ordered *pot de crème au chocolat* and coffee. All she had was tea. I began to feel a bit uneasy. Should I ask her if I'd talked a bit too long? Apologize? Still, after all, she could've interrupted, right?

"Did you argue *all* those cases?" Marcie asked (facetiously?).

"Of course not. But there's a new appeal I am consulting on. They're trying to define a Conscientious Objector. As a precedent, they're using *Webber* v. *Selective Service,* which I argued. Then I do some volunteer work—"

"You don't seem to ever stop," she said.

"Well, as Jimi Hendrix said at Woodstock, 'Things are pretty dirty and the world could use a scrubdown.' "

"Were you there?"

"No, I just read *Time* magazine to help me go to sleep."

"Oh," Marcie said.

Did that open syllable mean I'd disappointed her? Or was I

boring? Now that I looked back on this last hour (and a half!), I realized that I hadn't given her a chance to talk.

"What exactly do you do in fashion?" I inquired.

"Nothing socially uplifting. I'm with Binnendale's. You know the chain?"

Who doesn't know that golden chain of stores? That forty-carat lodestone for Conspicuous Consumers? Anyway, this tidbit clarified a lot. Miss Nash was obviously perfect for that flashy enterprise: so blond, so firm, so fully stacked, her Bryn Mawr elocution so mellifluous she probably could sell a handbag to a crocodile.

"I don't do that much selling," she replied as I continued with my awkward questioning. I'd figured her to be a sales trainee with grandiose ambitions.

"Then what exactly *do* you do?" I asked still more directly. This is how you break a witness down. Keep rephrasing questions that are basically the same.

"Hey, don't you get it up to here?" she said, her hand upon her slender throat. "Doesn't talking *anybody's* business bore you silly?"

She clearly meant that I'd been goddamn tedious.

"I hope my legal lecture didn't turn you off."

"No, honestly, I found it interesting. I only wish you'd said some more about yourself."

What could I say? I guessed the truth would be the best resort.

"There's nothing very pleasant I could tell you."

"Why?"

A pause. I looked into my coffee cup.

"I had a wife," I said.

"That's not unusual," she said. But sort of gently.

"She died."

There was a pause.

"I'm sorry," Marcie said.

"That's okay," I said. There is no other answer.

We then sat silently.

"I wish you'd told me sooner, Oliver."

"It's not all that easy."

"Doesn't talking help?"

"God, you're almost sounding like my shrink," I said.

"Oh," she said. "I thought I sounded like my own."

"Hey, what did you need shrinking for?" I asked, amazed that someone with such poise could possibly need doctorizing. "You didn't lose a wife."

That was a grim attempt at humor. Also unsuccessful.

"I lost a husband," Marcie said.

Oh, Barrett, with what grace you put your foot into your mouth!

"Jesus, Marcie," was the most I could say.

"Don't misconstrue," she quickly added. "It was only by divorce. But when we split our lives and our possessions, Michael got the confidence and I got all the hangups."

"Who was Mr. Nash?" I asked, immensely curious to know what kind of guy could snare this kind of girl.

"Can we change the subject, please?" she said. And sounded— so I thought—a trifle sad.

Curiously, I felt relieved that somewhere underneath her cool exterior Miss Marcie Nash had something that she couldn't talk about. Maybe even memories of hurt. That made her seem more human and her pedestal less lofty. Still, I didn't know what next to say.

Marcie did. "Oh, my, it's getting late."

My watch informed me that it was indeed ten forty-five. But still I thought that saying it right then meant I *had* turned her off.

"Check, please," she requested of the passing maître d'.

"Hey—no," I said. "I want to buy you dinner."

"Absolutely not. A deal's a deal."

True, at first I'd wanted her to pay. But now I felt so guilty for my gaucheries I had to expiate by treating her.

"I'll take the check, please," said yours truly, overruling her.

"Hey," objected Marcie. "We could wrestle, but we'd have to keep our clothes on and it wouldn't be much fun. So cool it, huh?" And then she said, "Dmitri?"

She knew the maître d' by name.

"Yes, ma'am?" Dmitri said.

"Please add a tip and sign for me."

"Of course, madam," he said, and greased off noiselessly.

I felt ill at ease. First she had upset me with the candid dinner talk. Then the mention of the naked wrestling (though by indirection) made me think: if she was sexually aggressive, how would I respond? And finally, she had her own account at "21"! Who was this girl?

"Oliver," she said, displaying all those perfect teeth, "I'll take you home."

"You will?"

"It's on my way," she said.

I couldn't hide it from myself. I was uptight about . . . the obvious.

"But, Oliver," she added with demureness and perhaps a tinge of irony, "because I bought you dinner doesn't mean you have to sleep with me."

"Oh, I'm much relieved," I said, pretending that I was pretending. "I wouldn't want to give you the impression I was loose."

"Oh, no," she said. "You're anything but loose."

In the taxicab as we were rocketing to my abode, a sudden thought occurred to me.

"Hey, Marcie," I said, as casually as possible.

"Yes, Oliver?"

"When you said my house was on your way—I hadn't told you where I lived."

"Oh, I just assumed you were an East Sixties type."

"And where do *you* live?"

"Not far from you," she said.

"That's nicely vague. And I suppose your phone's not listed either."

"No," she said. But offered neither explanation nor the number.

"Marcie?"

"Oliver?" Her tone was still unruffled and ingenuous.

"Why all the mystery?"

She reached across the cab and put her leather-gloved hand upon my nervous fist. She said, "Hang on there for a little bit, okay?"

Damn! Because there was no traffic at that hour, the taxi reached my place with speed uncommon—and right now much unappreciated.

"Wait a second," Marcie told the driver. I paused to hear if she might mention her next stop. But she was much too shrewd. She smiled at me, and with a tinsel brio murmured, "Thanks a lot."

"Oh, no," said I, aggressively genteel. "It's *I* who should thank *you.*"

There was a pause. I would be damned if I would beg for further scraps of information. So I left the cab.

"Hey, Oliver," she called, "more tennis Tuesday next?"

I was happy she suggested it. In fact, I showed too much by answering, "But that's a week from now. Why can't we play before?"

"Because I'll be in Cleveland," Marcie said.

"All that time?" I asked incredulously. "No one's *ever* spent a whole entire week in Cleveland!"

"Purge yourself of Eastern snobberies, my friend. I'll call you Monday evening to confirm the time. Good night, sweet prince."

Then, as if the cabby knew his *Hamlet*, he gunned off.

As I undid the third lock on my door, I started to get angry. What the hell was this?

And who the hell was she?

12

"Damn it all, she's hiding something."

"What's your fantasy?" asked Dr. London. Every time I'd make a simple realistic statement, he'd demand a flight of fancy. Even Freud described a concept called Reality!

"Look, Doctor, it is no delusion. Marcie Nash is conning me!"

"Mmm?"

He hadn't asked me why I was so exercised about a person I had barely met. I'd asked myself a lot and answered that I was competitive and simply didn't want to lose at Marcie's game (whatever it might be).

I then kept my patience and explained in detail to the doctor what I had discovered. I'd asked Anita, who's my very thorough secretary, to get Marcie on the phone ("Just wanted to say hi," I'd say). Naturally, my quarry hadn't told me where she would be staying. But Anita was a genius at locating people.

Binnendale's, whom she'd first telephoned, alleged they had no Marcie Nash among its personnel. But this did not dissuade Anita. She then called every possible hotel in greater Cleveland and the fashionable suburbs. When this didn't turn up any Marcie Nash, she tried motels and humbler hostelries. Nothing still. There absolutely was no Miss, Ms. or Madame Marcie Nash in the vicinity of Cleveland.

Therefore, Q.E.D. and damn it all, she's lying. Ergo she is somewhere else.

"What then," the doctor slowly asked, "is your . . . conclusion?"

"But it's not a fantasy!" I quickly said.

He did not demur. The case was opened and I started strong. I'd been brooding over it all day.

"First of all, it's obvious she's shacking up with someone. That's the only explanation for not giving me her phone and her address. Maybe she's still even married."

"Then why would she be seeing you?"

Christ, Dr. London was naïve. Or else behind the times. Or else ironic.

"I don't know. According to the articles I read, we're living in a liberated age. Maybe they just both agreed to 'open' their relationship."

"But if she's liberated, as you say, why doesn't she just tell you?"

"Aha, there lies the paradox. I figure Marcie's thirty—though she looks much younger. That means she's still a product of the early sixties—just like me. Things were not that loose and free back then. So, since the girls of Marcie's vintage still are more hung up than out, they tell you Cleveland when they're swinging in Bermuda."

"That's your fantasy?"

"Look, it could be Barbados," I conceded, "but she's on vacation with the guy she's living with. Who may or may not be her husband."

"And you're angry. . . ."

One did not need psychiatric training to discern that I was furious!

"Because she wasn't straight with me, goddammit!"

After bellowing, I wondered if the patient waiting outside leafing through the old *New Yorker*'s heard my blast.

I shut up for several seconds. Why did I get so excited in the process of convincing him I wasn't?

"Christ, I pity any guy that gets involved with such an uptight hypocrite."

A pause.

"'Involved'?" asked Dr. London, seizing my own adjective to use against me.

"No." I laughed. "I am extremely *un*involved. In fact, not only am I gonna write her off—I'm gonna send that bitch a telegram instructing her to go to hell."

Another pause.

"Except I can't," I then confessed. "I don't know her address."

I was in the midst of dreaming that I was asleep when—dammit —someone woke me on the telephone.

"Hi. Did I arouse, disturb or otherwise intrude?" The merry caller was Miss Marcie Nash. Her implication: was I having fun, or simply waiting doglike for her call.

"What I'm doing's strictly classified," I said, implying I was into some lubricious bit of grab-ass. "Where the hell are you?"

"I'm at the airport," she replied, as if it was the truth.

"Who're you with?" I asked quite casually, in hope she would be caught off guard.

"Some tired businessmen," she said.

I bet the business had been very tiring.

"Well, did you get a tan?" I asked.

"A what?" she said. "Hey, Barrett, are you smoking? Clear your head and tell me if we're playing tennis in the morning?"

I squinted at my wrist watch on the table. It was almost 1 A.M.

"It's already 'in the morning,'" I replied, annoyed by what she'd done all week compounded by her waking me. And not biting at my baited questions. And the whole continuing enigma.

"Do we play at six A.M.?" she asked. "Say yes or no."

I thought a lot for several miniseconds. Why the hell would she come back from fun and frolic in the tropics and yet want to go play tennis so damn early? Also, why not play with "roommate"? Was I just her tennis pro? Or did he have to breakfast with *his* wife? I ought to tell her off and go to sleep.

"Yeah, I'll be there," I said. Which wasn't quite what I'd intended.

I beat her to a pulp.

Next morning on the tennis court I showed no mercy whatsoever. I was wordless (save for "Are you ready?") and extremely vicious. Add to this the fact that Marcie's game was slightly off. She looked a trifle pale. Did it rain down in Bermuda? Or did she spend too much time indoors? Well, that was none of my concern.

"Heigh ho," she said with difficulty when the swift debacle ended. "Pancho didn't humor me today."

"I had a week to lose my sense of humor, Marcie."

"Why?"

"I thought the Cleveland joke was just a little much."

"What do you mean?" she said, and seemed ingenuous.

"Look, I'm too pissed off to even talk about it."

Marcie seemed confused. I mean she acted like she didn't have a clue that I was on to her.

"Hey, aren't we adults?" she said. "Why can't we talk about what's bugging you?"

"It isn't worth discussing, Marcie."

"Okay," she said, and sounded disappointed. "Obviously, you don't want to go to dinner."

"I was not aware there was a dinner."

"Isn't that supposed to be the prize?" she said.

I thought a moment. Should I tell her now? Or should I enjoy a lavish meal at her expense and *then* tell her to go to hell?

"Yeah—buy me a dinner," I replied, a trifle gruffly.

"When and where?" she said, apparently undaunted by my impoliteness.

"No, I'll just pick you up. At your place," I said pointedly.

"I won't be home," she answered. Yeah, a likely story.

"Marcie, I will pick you up if you're in Timbuktu."

"Okay, Oliver. I'll call you at your house around six-thirty and I'll tell you where I am."

"Suppose *I'm* not at home?" I said. A pretty cool riposte, I thought. To which I added, "Sometimes I have clients who invite me to their offices in outer space."

"Okay, I'll keep calling till your rocket lands."

She started toward the ladies' locker room and turned. "Oliver, you know I'm starting to believe you're really crazy?"

"Hey, I won a big one."

Dr. London offered no congratulations. Yet he knew the action was significant since I'd referred to it in sessions past. So once again I had to abstract *Channing* v. *Riverbank*. The latter is the fancy condominium on East End Avenue, the former, Charles F. Channing, Jr., president of Magnitex, a former Penn State All-American, a prominent Republican . . . and also eminently black. His application for the purchase of the penthouse was denied for some odd reason. And that reason brought him to seek counsel. He chose J & M for our prestige. Old man Jonas gave his case to me.

We won it easily, invoking not the recent open housing laws—which have some ambiguities—but simply citing *Jones* v. *Mayer*, last year argued in the high court (392 U.S. 409). Herein the justices affirmed that 1866's civil rights act guaranteed to everyone the freedom to buy property. It was soundly rooted in the First Amendment. Riverbank was soundly routed. And my client moves in on the thirtieth.

"For once I even made some money for the firm," I added. "Channing is a millionaire."

But London still withheld all comment.

"Old man Jonas took me out to lunch. Marsh—the other half—came by for coffee. They were hinting at a partnership. . . ."

Still no comment. What exactly would impress this guy?

"I'm seducing Marcie Nash tonight!"

Aha. He coughed.

"Don't you wonder why?" I asked, my tone demanding a response.

He answered quietly. "You like her."

I began to laugh. He didn't understand. I then explained this was the only way to get the answers. Crude as it may sound (and cynical), seduction is a potent way to truth. And when I've learned what Marcie has been hiding, I'll just tell her off, depart, and feel terrific.

Now if London dares to ask me for a fantasy, I'll walk right out.

He didn't. And instead he made me ask myself why I had been so self-congratulating. Why had I been strutting verbally like some damn peacock? Was my emphasis on legal triumph just to draw attention from some other . . . insecurities?

Of course not. Why should I be insecure?

She's just a girl.

Or isn't that the problem?

"Hey, I'm naked, Marcie."

"What is that supposed to mean?"

"You caught me in the shower."

"Shall I call you back? I wouldn't interrupt your monthly ritual."

"Never mind," I snarled, ignoring her remark. "Just tell me where the hell you are."

"The White Plains shopping center. In Binnendale's."

"Then be outside the front in twenty minutes and I'll pick you up."

"Oliver," she said, "it's fifteen miles away!"

"All right," I casually replied. "I'll pick you up in *fifteen* minutes."

"But, Oliver, please do me one small favor."

"What?" I said.

"Put on your clothes."

Thanks to the mechanical perfection of my Targa 911S and also to my driving creativity (I even pass on center strips—the cops are always too impressed to stop me), I zoomed into the shopping center twenty-seven minutes later.

Marcie Nash was waiting (posing?) just where I had told her to. She had a package in her hand. Her figure looked—if possible —more perfect than the other night.

"Hello," she said. As I leaped out, she came and kissed me on the cheek. And put the package in my hand. "Here's a little gift to mollify and butter you. And, by the way, I like your car."

"It likes you too," I said.

"Then let me drive."

Oh, not my little Porsche. I couldn't. . . .

"Next time, Marcie," I said.

"Come on, I know the way," she said.

"To where?"

"To where we're going. Please . . ."

"Marcie, no. It's much too delicate an instrument."

"Don't sweat," she said while climbing into the driver's seat. "Your instrument will be in expert hands."

And I confess it was. She drove like Jackie Stewart. Only he would never take a hairpin turn as fast as Marcie did. Frankly, I confess to intermittent trepidation. And some total fear.

"Do you like it?" Marcie asked.

"What?" I said, pretending not to notice the speedometer.

"Your present," Marcie said.

Oh, yeah. I had forgotten all about the butter-up. My panicked fingers were still clutching that unopened offering.

"Hey, unscrew your digits—open up and take a look."

It was a soft black cashmere sweater with Alfa Romeo emblazoned on the chest. In vivid red.

"It's Emilio Ascarelli. He's the new Italian whiz kid."

Clearly Marcie had the money to afford this kind of thing. But why'd she buy it? Guilt, I guess.

"Hey, this is gorgeous, Marcie. Thanks a lot."

"I'm pleased you're pleased," she said. "Part of my business is to guess the public's taste."

"Ah, you're a hooker," I replied, with tiny smile to punctuate my witticism.

"Isn't everybody?" Marcie said. With charm. And grace.

And maybe truth?

One may well ask, since I'd been recently a bit uncertain of myself, how could I be so sure I would seduce Miss Marcie Nash.

Because it's easier without emotional involvement. I know by definition making love implies affection. But often nowadays the act is merely a competitive event. In this regard I felt completely comfortable—psyched up, in fact—to handle Marcie Nash.

And yet the more I paid attention to the comely driver and forgot to watch the dash, the thoughts that London had evoked came back to me. Notwithstanding all the mystery and my ostensible hostility, did not I maybe slightly *like* this girl? And was I maybe faking myself out in order to reduce anxiety?

For was it really possible, once having made most tender love with Jenny Cavilleri, to dichotomize? Could I divide the act of love, be sensual yet insincere?

People can and do. As I would prove.

For in my present state, without involvement was the *only* way I thought I could.

Guidebooks give Le Méchant Loup in Bedford Hills an "adequate" for its cuisine. But for its rustic atmosphere and lodgings it receives an "excellent." Nestled (as they say) within the green and tranquil trees, it offers an escape from all the pressures of our urban lives.

What the guidebooks need not even mention is Le Méchant Loup is perfect for a shack-up. Dinner may just barely pass, but up the stairs awaits the atmosphere that critics praise. Learning this would be our destination, I concluded that my chances for success were . . . "excellent."

Yet in a way I was annoyed.

Who had chosen this locale? And who had made the reservation on whose own without consulting whom? And who was driving there so swiftly in *my* lovely Porsche?

We turned off the highway, entering a forest with a narrow road which seemed to stretch for miles. At last a light shone up ahead. A lantern. And the sign: LE MÉCHANT LOUP, A COUNTRY INN.

Marcie slowed (at last) and turned into the courtyard. In the moonlight, all I could distinguish was the outline of a Swiss chalet. Visible within were two huge fireplaces flickering illumination on a dining room and living room. Nothing glimmered in the floors above. As we crossed the parking lot, I noticed but a single other car, a white Mercedes SLC. The place would not be overpopulated. Surely conversation could be . . . intimate.

"Hope the food is worth the drive," I quipped (ho ho).

"Hope you won't be disappointed," Marcie said. And took my arm as we went in.

They sat us at a table by the fireplace. I ordered drinks.

"One orange juice and a carafe of any cheapo California white that isn't Gallo."

"Cesar Chavez would be proud of you," said Marcie, as the waitress bustled off. "You should make her check to see the oranges are union-picked."

"I'm not a watchdog for your morals, Marcie."

Then I looked around. We were the only people there.

"Are we too early?" I inquired.

"I think because it's so far out, the people mostly come on weekends."

"Oh," I said. And though I'd told myself I shouldn't ask, I asked: "Have you been here before?"

"No," Marcie said. But I figured she was lying.

"Why'd you pick it sight unseen?"

"I heard it was romantic. And it *is* romantic, don't you think?"

"Oh . . . excellent," I said. And took her hand.

"They've got a fireplace in every upstairs room," she said.

"Sounds cool," I said.

"Sounds warm to me." She smiled.

A silence. Then as casually as possible I queried, "Are we also booked on high?"

She nodded yes. And added, "Just in case."

I wondered why I wasn't as elated as I thought I should be.

"Just in case of what?" I asked.

"Of snow," she said. And squeezed my hand.

The waitress brought us Marcie's glass and my carafe. The fire joining forces with the wine now warmed in me the feeling of my Right to Know.

"Say, Marcie, in what name did you reserve?"

"Donald Duck," she answered, poker-faced.

"No, really, Marcie. I'm curious to know the names you pick for checking into different places."

"Oh?"

"Like Cleveland, for example."

"Are we back to Cleveland?" Marcie said.

"Just how were you registered in Cleveland?" lawyer Barrett barreled in.

"Actually, I wasn't," she replied. Unhesitatingly. And unabashedly.

Aha!

"I mean I didn't stay in a hotel," she added casually.

Oho?

"But were you actually there?"

She crinkled up her mouth.

"Oliver," she said after a moment. "What's the purpose of this inquisition?"

I smiled. I poured another glass, refueling in midair. And tried a different line of questioning.

"Marcie, friends should level with each other, don't you think?" That had seemed effective. My use of "friends" evoked a spark.

"Obviously," Marcie said.

Perhaps my flattery, my quiet tone of voice, softened her. And so I asked directly, showing no scintilla of emotional involvement:

"Marcie, are you hiding certain facts about yourself?"

"I really was in Cleveland, Oliver," she said.

"Okay, but are you camouflaging other things?"

There was a pause.

And then she nodded yes.

See, I was right. The air was clear at last. Or clearing, anyway. And yet the rest was silence. Marcie simply sat there and withheld all further comment. Yet now something of her aura of serene self-confidence had visibly diminished. She looked almost vulnerable. I felt a twinge of sympathy. Which I suppressed.

"Well . . . ?" I said.

She reached across the table and she touched my hand. "Hey, look. I know, I've been evasive. But please take it easy. I'll come through."

What was that supposed to mean? Her hand remained on mine.

"Can we order dinner?" Marcie said.

What now? I asked myself. Settle for a slight postponement? Run the risk of never getting back to where we were: the verge of truth?

"Marcie, can we cover one or two more little topics first?"

She hesitated. Then replied, "If you insist."

"Please help me put the pieces of a puzzle in their place, okay?" She simply nodded. And I launched into a summary of the incriminating evidence.

"What would one conclude about a lady who gave no address or phone? Who traveled and sojourned in unknown places incognito? Who never specified—indeed avoided—all discussion of her occupation?"

Marcie offered no assistance. "What do you conclude?" she asked.

"You're shacking up with someone," I said. Calmly and without recrimination.

She smiled a slightly nervous smile. And shook her head.

"Or else you're married. Or he's married."

She looked at me.

"Am I supposed to check the answer on your questionnaire?"

"Yes."

"None of the above."

Like hell, I thought.

"Why would I be seeing you?" she asked.

"Your contract's nonexclusive."

She did not seem flattered.

"Oliver, I'm not that kind of person."

"All right, then what kind *are* you?"

"I don't know," she said. "A little insecure."

"You're full of shit."

That was uncalled for. And I instantly regretted saying it.

"Is that a sample of your courtroom manner, Mr. Barrett?"

"No," I said politely. "But here I couldn't nail you down for perjury."

"Oliver, stop being such a creep! A marginally nice and not too unattractive woman throws herself right at you. And instead of acting like a normal man, you play the Grand Inquisitor!"

That "normal" zinger really sliced me. What a bitch. "Look, if you don't like it, Marcie, you can call it off."

"I didn't notice anything was *on*. But if you feel the sudden need to go to court—or church—or to a monastery—*go!*"

"With pleasure," I replied, and rose.

"Good-bye," she said.

"Good-bye," I said. But neither of us moved.

"Go on—I'll take the check," she said. And waved me off as if I was a fly.

But I would not be shooed.

"Hey, look, I'm not a total bastard. I won't leave you all alone here, miles from nowhere."

"Please don't be gallant. I've got a car outside."

Again a valve exploded in my brain. I'd caught this bitch red-handed in another lie!

"You claimed you'd never been here, Marcie. How the hell'd your car arrive—remote control?"

"Oliver," she said, now flushed with anger, "it is none of your damn paranoiac business. But to set you on your way, I'll simply tell you that a guy I work with dropped it off. Because regardless of the outcome of our rendezvous, I have to be in Hartford in the morning."

"Why Hartford?" I demanded, though it really wasn't any of my business.

"Because my fancy lover wants to buy me some insurance!" Marcie shouted. "Now go soak your head."

I'd really gone too far too fast. I was confused. I mean I sensed that we should both stop shouting and sit down. But then we'd just exchanged a violent set of "go to hells." And so I *had* to go.

A summer rain was falling as I fumbled trying to unlock my car.

"Hey—can we take a drive around the block?"

Marcie was behind me, looking very solemn. She had left the inn without a coat or anything.

"No, Marcie," I replied. "We've already gone around in far too many circles." I unlocked the car.

"Oliver, I've got a reason."

"Oh, I'm sure you do."

"You didn't give me half a chance."

"You didn't give me half a truth."

I got in and closed the door. Marcie stood there as I revved the motor. Motionless and staring at me. As I slowly passed her, I rolled down the window.

"Will you call me?" she said quietly.

"You forget," I answered, with no little irony, "I haven't got your number. Think of that."

At which I shifted gears and gunned it from the courtyard to the road.

And thence to New York City, to forget Miss Marcie Nash forever.

16

"What were you frightened of?"

This was Dr. London's only comment after I'd recounted everything.

"I never said that I was frightened."

"But you ran off."

"Look, it became as clear as day that Marcie was a not so nice girl on the make."

"You mean seducing you?"

He was naïve.

"'On the make,'" I then explained as patiently as possible, "because my name is Barrett, and it doesn't take much research to discover that I come from money."

There. I'd made my point. Now there was silence in the court.

"You don't believe that," Dr. London said at last. His certainty that I was not convinced forced me to think again.

"I guess I don't," I said.

There was another silence.

"All right, you're the doctor. What exactly *did* I feel?"

"Oliver," said London. "You are here precisely to improve communications with yourself." He asked again, "How did you feel?"

"A little vulnerable."

"And . . . ?"

"A little scared."

"Of what?"

I couldn't answer right away. In fact, I was incapable of answering out loud. I *was* afraid. But not because I thought she'd tell me: "Yeah, I'm living with an all-star fullback who's a Ph.D. in astrophysics and who turns me on."

No. I rather think that I was scared of hearing:

"Oliver, I like you."

Which would shake me up much more.

Granted Marcie was a mystery. But she was neither Mata Hari nor the whore of Babylon. Indeed, her single fault was that she didn't have an obvious, convenient fault. (I'd had to find her one!) And Marcie's lies, whatever may have prompted them, did not excuse the falsehood that I told myself. That I was not . . . involved.

Because I nearly was. I very nearly was.

That's why I panicked and I fled. Because in *almost* liking someone else I felt disloyal to the only girl I ever loved.

But how much longer could I live this way, forever on my guard lest human feelings catch me unaware? In point of fact, my turmoil now was multiplied. And I was torn by two dilemmas.

One: How could I deal with memories of Jenny?

Two: How could I find Marcie Nash?

17

"Barrett, you're a fucking lunatic!"

"Be quiet, Simpson!" I retorted as I motioned frantically for him to keep his voice down.

"What's the matter—will I wake the tennis balls?" he growled. He was disgusted and confused.

And with good reason. It was barely 6 A.M. I'd dragged him from his duties at the hospital to be my stooge at Gotham Tennis Club.

"Oh, Barrett," Simpson whined, while changing from his doctor whites to tennis whites I had provided, "tell me one more time why this is so important!"

"It's a favor, Steve," I said. "I need a partner I can trust."

He didn't understand. I hadn't told him everything.

"Hey, look," he said, "we run whenever I can break away. I can't devote my life to furthering your masochism. Why at *dawn*, goddammit?"

"Please," I said. So earnestly that Simpson sympathized. At least he shut his mouth.

We ambled very slowly from the locker room. He from his tiredness and I from calculation.

"We're number six," said Steve. And yawned.

"I know," I said. And as we headed there, I scrutinized the population of courts one through five. But no familiar face.

We batted balls till 8 A.M., with Simpson barely staying on his feet. And begging me to let him quit. I wasn't too adroit myself.

"You played like cottage cheese," he puffed. "You must be overtired too."

"Yeah, yeah," I said. And wondered where she was. In Cleveland maybe?

"Steve, I gotta ask a giant favor."

"What?" he asked, suspicion in his eyes.

"Another game. Tomorrow."

From my tone and pleading Simpson felt my urgency.

"Okay. But not at six A.M."

"That's just the point," I said. "It's *gotta* be at six again!"

"No, goddammit, there are limits!" Simpson snarled. And punched the locker in frustration.

"Please," I said. And then confessed, "Steve, there's a girl involved."

His weary eyes now widened. "Yeah?" he said.

I nodded yes. And told him that I met her at the club and knew no other way of finding her.

Simpson looked relieved that I was interested in someone. And agreed to play. Then he thought of something: "What if she's not here tomorrow too?"

"We'll just have to keep on coming till she is."

He merely shrugged. A friend in need, if an exhausted friend indeed.

At the office I kept badgering Anita. Even if I only left my desk to heed the call of nature, I'd come charging back demanding, "Any calls?"

And when she went for lunch, I'd order in a sandwich. Thus I kept a constant watch upon the telephone (I didn't trust that new kid at the switchboard). I wouldn't miss when Marcie called.

Except she didn't.

Wednesday afternoon I had to go to court to argue a motion for a preliminary injunction. This took almost two whole hours. I got back around a quarter after five.

"Any calls, Anita?"

"Yeah."

"Well . . . *what?*"

"Your doctor. He's at home this evening after eight."

What could this be? Did London—whom I couldn't see that day—think I was cracking?

"What *exactly* was the message?"

"Jesus, Oliver, I told you! She just said—"

"What *she?*"

"Just let me finish, would you? She just said to tell you, 'Dr. Stein will be at home this evening!' "

"Dr. Stein . . ." I said, betraying disappointment. It had been Joanna.

"Who were you expecting—Dr. Jonas Salk?" Anita asked.

I reflected for a minisecond. Maybe what I needed was a friendly conversation with a human being like Joanna. No, that would be unfair. She's too . . . together for a guy like me.

"And nothing else?" I snarled.

"I left some memos. Interoffice. Okay if I leave?"

"Yeah, yeah."

I hurried to my desk. As might have been expected, interoffice memos in a law firm all related to assorted cases that the firm was handling. Not a word from Marcie.

Two days later, old man Jonas asked me to his office for a meeting. Damn. I told Anita I would buy her lunch if she would stay on guard. The boss had brought me in—again with Mr. Marsh—to talk about the case of Harold Baye, a wiretapper for the FBI who had discovered he himself was being bugged by his own bureau. Insects of this sort were now a veritable plague. Harold had hairy tales to tell about surveillance of some White House staff. Naturally, he didn't have much dough. But Jonas thought the firm should take his case "to tune the public in."

The second that our meeting broke, I sprinted back.

"Any calls, Anita?"

"Washington, D.C.," she said, kind of impressed at having taken such a message. "The director of the OEO."

"Oh," I said, not quite enthusiastic. "Nothing else?"

"Were you expecting maybe Jacqueline Onassis?"

"Hey, look—don't kid around, Anita," I retorted frostily. And stomped into my office.

I overheard Anita mutter, honestly confused, "What's *eating* him?"

Naturally, I wasn't merely passive, waiting for a call. I played tennis every morning. When poor Simpson couldn't make it, I took "lessons" from old Petie Clark, their antiquated pro.

"*Let me tell you, sonny, Petie's taught 'em all. They go from me to Wimbledon.*"

"*Hey, did you ever teach a Marcie Nash?*"

"*You mean that pretty little gal—*"

"*Yeah, yeah.*"

"*—who won the doubles with that red-haired fella back in '48?*"

"*Never mind. Forget it, Petie.*"

"*Tell the truth, I don't remember if I taught that one or not.*"

And every afternoon I ran. Against the traffic, so I'd get a better look at faces. Still no luck. Whatever Marcie did, it sometimes took her out of town for many days. But I would persevere.

Though I had immediately joined the Gotham Tennis Club (the sole criterion for membership is money), they would not cooperate. I mean the office would vouchsafe no information whatsoever on my fellow clubbees.

"*You mean you haven't got a list?*"

"*It's just for office use. I'm sorry, Mr. Barrett.*"

In a moment of frustration, I considered asking Harold Baye to bug their phone. But then I stopped myself. Still, that's an index of my desperate state of mind.

Obviously, I inquired at Binnendale's. With some fishy story of an aunt and an inheritance, I learned that they did, in fact, have three employees with the surname Nash. I checked them personally.

First, in Ladies' Shoes, I met Priscilla Nash. She was a friendly woman who had worked there over forty years. She'd never married. And her only living relative was Uncle Hank in Georgia and her only friend a cat named Agamemnon. To obtain this information cost me eighty-seven bucks. I had to purchase boots, "a birthday present for my sister," as I chatted amiably with Miss Nash. (I got Anita's size; the gift just added to her schizophrenia.)

Then to **Mr. B.**, their with-it men's department. There to meet Miss Elvy Nash. "Hello," said Elvy, flashing lots of charm and chic. This Nash was black and very beautiful. "What can I do you for today?" she smiled. Oh, what indeed!

Miss Elvy Nash persuaded me that guys were really into shirt-and-sweater combinations. Before I knew it I was holding six of them. And she was ringing up—would you believe?—three hundred dollars and some change. "Now the chicks won't keep their hands off you. You'll look as fine as wine," Miss Elvy said. And I departed looking good. But still, unfortunately, looking.

Happily for my finances, the third and final Nash was Rodney P., a buyer who had been in Europe for the last six weeks.

"Where does that leave you?" Steve asked, heroically continuing to join me for the early morning matches.

"Nowhere," I replied.

Also I was plagued by a recurrent nightmare.

I kept reliving that excruciating fight I had with Jenny in the first year we were married. She had wanted me to see my father, or at least to make my peace by telephone. I'm still chagrined at how I yelled at her. I was a madman. Frightened, Jenny fled to god-knows-where. I sprinted madly, turning everything in Cambridge upside down. But couldn't find her. Then at last in panic I came home and found her waiting on the outside steps.

That was my dream exactly, save for one detail: Jenny didn't reappear.

I searched as frantically as ever. I returned in desperation as I had. *But Jenny wasn't there at all.*

What was that supposed to mean?

That I was scared of losing Jenny?

Or that I wanted (!) to lose Jenny?

Dr. London offered a suggestion: Was I not of late involved in yet another quest for yet another lady after yet another fit of anger?

Yes. I was in search of Marcie Nash.

But what does Marcie have to do with Jenny?

Nothing, naturally.

Three weeks later, I gave up. Marcie-with-the-unknown-second-name would never call. And who could really blame her? Meanwhile I was very near collapse from my athletic schedule. Not to mention endless finger-tapping, waiting for that phone to ring. Needless to report, my legal work was lousy—when I got around to doing any. Everything was going to hell. Except my mood, which was already there. This would have to stop. So on the three-week anniversary of the Massacre at Méchant Loup, I said, That's it, the case is closed. Tomorrow I return to sanity. And to commemorate this great occasion, I decided to play hooky for the afternoon.

"Oliver, where can I reach you if I need you?" asked Anita, who was also near a breakdown from my ceaseless and bizarre demands for messages that never came.

"No one needs me," I replied, and left the office.

Henceforth, as I walked uptown, I would no longer suffer from hallucinations. Fantasies of seeing Marcie just ahead. Naturally they always turned out to be yet another tall and slender blonde. Once I even saw one with a tennis racket. How I sprinted (I was in such splendid shape), only to be wrong again. Yet another almost-Marcie. New York City teems with her facsimiles.

Now when I reached the Fifties, I would go by Binnendale's department store precisely as I had before my three-week malady. Dispassionate. The mind on lofty thoughts like legal precedents or what I'd have for dinner. No more costly explorations, no more systematic cruising of the various departments in hopes of glimpsing Marcie in the Tennis Shop or maybe Lingerie. Now I'd simply glance at what the windows pitched, and move on by.

But hey, since last I looked—that is, since yesterday—there'd been some changes. One new decoration seized my eye: EXCLUSIVE—JUST ARRIVED FROM ITALY. THE LATEST BY EMILIO ASCARELLI.

And on the handsome shoulders of a Yalie-looking dummy was a cashmere sweater. Black. Emblazoned Alfa Romeo. But the window's claim that this exclusive item just arrived was perjury. My body could refute it in an instant. For by chance (or maybe not by chance) I had that sweater on right now. And I'd received it several weeks ago. Three weeks, to be precise.

At last a solid clue! Whoever handled imports must have sold or given one to Marcie in advance. I maybe now could storm the citadel, decked out in evidence, demanding and receiving instant answers.

But hold it, Oliver. You said the frenzy's over and it is. Move on. The goddamn cashmere case is closed.

I was at home some minutes later, going through my vast collection of athletic garments, with a view to running in the park. I'd narrowed down the choice of socks to three or four ungrungy ones (or relatively speaking), when the phone rang.

Let it ring. I have priorities.

It wouldn't stop. Probably Anita with some trivia from Washington.

I picked it up to cut it off.

"Barrett isn't here!" I growled.

"Oh? Is he with his clients up in outer space?"

Marcie.

"Uh—" (How's that for eloquence?)

"What are you doing, Oliver?" she said. Quite softly.

"I was just about to run in Central Park," I said.

"Too bad. I would have joined you. But I ran this morning."

Ah, that explained her recent absence in the afternoons.

"Oh," I said. And quickly added, "That's too bad."

"I called your office, just to ask you if you'd had lunch. But if you're going running—"

"No," I quickly said. "I'm sorta hungry."

A little pause.

"That's good," she said.

"Where should we meet?" I asked.

"Would you come and pick me up?"

Would I *what?*

"Where are you, Marcie?"

"At Binnendale's. The business offices on top. Just ask for—"

"Yeah. Okay. What time?"

"Don't rush. At your convenience. I'll be waiting."

"Okay."

And we both hung up at once.

Quandary: Should I sprint immediately? Or did I have time to shave and shower?

Compromise: Perform ablutions, then take taxi to make up lost time.

In fifteen minutes I was back at Binnendale's.

I wanted to race up the stairs, but figured that appearing through the fire doors would not be cool. So I took the elevator. Up to the very top.

At the summit, I emerged into a veritable paradise. Carpet like a huge expanse of virgin beach—and just as soft. Up the shore there sat a secretary. And behind her was America. I mean a map of the United States with little flags to indicate where Binnendale's had staked their claims.

"May I help you, sir?" the secretary said.

"Uh . . . yes. My name is Barrett—"

"Yes. You want Marcie," she replied.

"Uh . . . that's correct."

"Just take that corridor," she said, "and go straight down. I'll say that you're en route."

I quickly hit the corridor, then told myself slow down. Walk, do not run. As slow as possible. (I only wish I could decelerate my heart.)

It was a lush cocoonlike tunnel. Where the hell would it end up? Anyway, the neighborhood seemed fairly good.

First I passed by William Ashworth's office (General Merchandise Manager).

Then Arnold H. Sundel, the Treasurer.

Then Stephen Nichols, Jr., First Vice-President.

At last the passage opened out. And in the wide expanse before me sat two secretaries.

Behind them as I neared, a portal opened.

There she was.

I stopped.

Marcie looked at me and I at her. I couldn't think of anything appropriate to say.

"Come in," she said (she clearly won the prize for poise).

I followed her inside. The room was large and elegant.

No one else was there.

Only then could I appreciate why she was all alone.

Finally she spoke.

"It's been a miserable three weeks."

"Not business-wise," I answered. "I've gone bankrupt shopping here to try and find you."

Marcie smiled a little.

"Look," I said, attempting an apology, "I guess I was a little too precipitous."

"I helped precipitate," she said. "I was a little too mysterious." But now the mystery was solved.

"You don't exactly work for Binnendale's," I said. "It works for you."

She nodded. Almost in embarrassment.

"I should have told you sooner," Marcie said.

"That's okay. I understand now." She seemed enormously relieved.

"Hey, Marce, you can't imagine just how *well* I understand the syndrome. When you're rich that inner demon's always asking, 'Do they like me for myself or just my dough?' That sound familiar?"

I looked at her.

"That's sort of it," she said.

I wanted to say more. Like, Hey, you're really beautiful. You're bright. You've got a thousand qualities that any guy would groove on. But I couldn't. Yet.

Someone had to make some kind of move. And so I did.

"Let's get out of here," I said.

She nodded, rummaged in her top desk drawer, withdrew a key. And tossed it to me.

"It's downstairs," she said.

"You mean I get to drive?" said I, agreeably amazed. She smiled and nodded yes.

"But please be careful, Oliver. My instrument is no less delicate than yours."

19

I'd vaguely read about it several years ago. The sudden death of founding father Walter Binnendale. How he'd bequeathed his great eleven-city kingdom to a daughter who was then ridiculously young.

Once upon a time there'd been an older brother. But as racing fans recall, in 1965 "Bin" Binnendale spun off the track and crashed at Zandvoort, only seconds after overtaking Boissier for the lead. Hence Marcie had become the only heir. Knowledgeable press reports suggested that the little girl would sell the stores as soon as possible and live the life a golden heiress should. Instead, this twenty-four-year-old thought she would dabble in tycooning and took over Daddy's job.

The experts smiled. Her "leadership" would surely bring the chain to rapid ruin. And yet it didn't tumble all that quickly. Two years later, Binnendale's proposed expansion to the West. Again, the trade dismissed it as an adolescent folly. By the time they opened in Los Angeles (branch seventeen), their stock had doubled. Maybe it was just dumb luck, but those now smiling did so to her face.

Now and then I'd come across some tiny notice of the Binnendale financial progress. When her name appeared at all, the president was mentioned inconspicuously. Never did they print her picture. Never did the social pages trumpet her activities. "People" columns did not chronicle her marriage. None reported her divorce. Such anonymity is near impossible when you're among the richest people in the country. Not to mention blond and beautiful. It therefore came as no surprise to learn that Marcie paid an agency to keep the press away.

This and other tidbits were imparted to me as I drove her white Mercedes northward on the Merritt Parkway. First I'd used her telephone to cancel Dr. London. Then she called her office to say "Screw my afternoon appointments" (in so many words). Finally, I yanked the plug out.

Marcie smiled benignly as I willfully destroyed her private property.

"For some unfathomable reason, Oliver, I like you. But you are impossibly impulsive."

"You're not too possible yourself," I answered. "Think of all the grief you could have spared us if you'd only said right on the track, 'My name is Binnendale.' I would have said, 'So what? That's not as fascinating as your ass.'"

A certain luminescence in her eyes said she believed me.

"Look, Oliver, I know I'm slightly paranoid. But just remember I've been hurt."

"Just what exactly did your husband do?"

"To me? To other girls? Please be specific."

"What's he doing now, for instance?"

"Nothing."

"Nothing?"

"Well, let's put it this way: he is very . . . 'settled down.'" Her tone was strange. She couldn't possibly have meant what I imagined.

"Marce, you don't imply you had to . . . pay him?"

"No," she said, "I don't imply. I state. He's now a wealthy divorcé."

I was astounded. How could Marcie of all people have been so amazingly faked out?

I didn't ask. She *wanted* me to hear.

"Look," she said, "I was a college senior, wondering just what the hell my role in life would be. Then—presto! Enter this extremely charismatic, very handsome guy . . ."

I wished she hadn't emphasized his looks.

". . . who told me all the things I wanted to believe." She paused.

"I was a kid," she said. "I fell incredibly in love."

"And then?"

"Well, Father was still hoping to get Bin to take his helmet off and join the business. Naturally, my brother just accelerated in the opposite direction. So when suddenly I show up with my flashy boyfriend, Father absolutely flipped. He thought Mike was Jesus Christ and Einstein—only with a neater haircut! I mean, even if I'd wanted to, I couldn't have cast doubts on Michael's sheer perfection. Anyway, I think my father loved me most when I delivered this terrific second son. At the wedding I was half expecting *him* to say, 'I do.'"

"But how did Bin react?"

"Oh, it was loathing at first sight. They hated one another. Bin kept telling me that Michael was 'a barracuda in a J. Press suit.'"

"Which, I take it, he turned out to be."

"Well, that's a bit unkind. I mean to barracudas."

She had clearly tried these bitter jokes before. And failed to make the situation anything but sad.

"But what exactly made you ultimately split?" I asked.

"Michael didn't like me."

Marcie tried to speak as if it didn't hurt.

"What specifically?"

"I think he realized that much as Walter liked him, Bin would someday just show up and be the boss. Since Michael wasn't born to be an understudy, he just threw the towel in."

"Too bad," I tried to quip.

"Yeah. If only he had waited five more months . . ." Her narrative now ended. With no further comment. Even without wishing Michael Nash would rot in hell.

I had no notion what to say ("Gee, sorry you got screwed"?) And so I simply drove. We listened to an eight-track Joan Baez.

And then a thought occurred to me.

"Hey, Marcie, what exactly made you think I might be different?"

"Nothing. I just hoped you would be."

Then she touched my arm, inducing a most pleasant physical sensation in my spine as well. Things were progressing from the purely spiritual. So let's have a full disclosure.

"Marcie, have you ever given any thought to *my* last name?"

"No. Should I have?" And then it dawned on her.

"Barrett . . . the investment bank? The mills? Is that your family?"

"A distant relative," I said. "My father."

We rode in silence for a while. Then she said quietly, "I didn't know." Which, I confess, made *me* feel good.

On we drove, into the velvet darkness of New England.

Not that I was stalling. Merely looking for a really special place.

"I think we need a fire, Marce."

"Yes, Oliver."

It took us till Vermont to find the perfect setting. Uncle Abner's Cabins. On a little lake called Kenawaukee. Sixteen-fifty for the night. Including firewood. The nearest place for dining was a local bistro down the road. Called Howard Johnson's.

Thus before our fireside embracings I took Marcie for a lavish meal at HoJo's.

Over dinner we exchanged our childhoods.

First I bored her with my competition-admiration for my father. Then she sang the second chorus of that song to me. Every move she ever made in life was always as a challenge or a message to her own Big Daddy.

"Frankly, it was only when my brother died that Walter seemed to notice me at all."

We were like two actors analyzing our performances in different *Hamlets*. Only what amazed me was that Marcie hadn't played Ophelia. Her role, like mine, had been the Melancholy

Prince. I had always thought that women's rivalry was with their mothers. Apropos of which, she hadn't mentioned Mummy once.

"Did you have a mother?" I inquired.

"Yes," she said. Without emotion.

"Is she still alive?" I asked.

She nodded yes.

"She and Walter split in 1956. She didn't ask for custody. She married a developer in San Diego."

"Do you ever see her?"

"She was at the wedding."

Marcie's little smile could not convince me that she didn't care.

"I'm sorry that I asked."

"I would have told you anyway," she said. "Now *you*."

"What?"

"Tell me something terrible about your past." I thought a minute. And confessed.

"I was a dirty hockey player."

"Really?" Marcie flashed.

"Uh-huh."

"I want the *details*, Oliver!"

She really did. Half an hour later she was still demanding hockey stories.

But I then lightly put my hand upon her lips.

"Tomorrow, Marce," I said.

As I was paying, she remarked, "Hey, Oliver, this was the nicest meal I ever had." I somehow think she didn't mean the macaroni or the hot fudge sundae.

Afterward we walked back hand in hand to Uncle Abner's.

And then built a fire.

And then helped each other not be shy when we both were.

And later in the evening did some more nice things much less self-consciously.

And fell asleep in one another's arms.

Marcie woke at dawn. But I was out already, sitting by the lake to watch the sun come up. Bundled in her coat, her hair all tousled, she sat next to me and whispered (though there wasn't anyone for miles).

"How do you feel?"

"Okay," I answered, reaching for her hand. But knowing also that my eyes and voice revealed a trace of sadness.

"Do you feel . . . uneasy, Oliver?"

I nodded that I sort of did.

"Because you thought of . . . Jenny?"

"No," I said, and looked out toward the lake. "Because I didn't."

Then, forsaking verbal conversation, we stood up and walked back down to Howard Johnson's for a massive breakfast.

"What are your feelings?"

"Jesus, can't you tell?"

I was grinning like an idiot. What other symptoms could confirm the diagnosis I was happy—pirouettes around the doctor's office?

"I can't put it medically. Your science seems to lack the terminology for joy."

Still no answer. Couldn't London say at least "Congratulations"?

"Doctor, I am high! Like a flag on the fourth of July!"

Sure I knew the words were trite. But hell, I was excited, anxious to discuss. Well, not discuss—just crow about it. After endless months of numbness, here at last was something that resembled human sensibility. How could I put it so that a psychiatrist could get the message?

"Look, we *like* each other, Doctor. A relationship is in the making. Blood is flowing in a former statue."

"Those are headlines," Dr. London offered.

"It's the essence," I insisted. "Don't you fathom that I'm feeling good?"

There was a pause. Why was it he could so well comprehend my prior pain and now seemed so obtuse to my euphoria? I looked straight at him for an answer.

All he said was: "Five o'clock tomorrow."

I bounced up and bounded out.

We'd left Vermont at seven forty-five and, stopping twice for coffee, gas and kisses, reached her baroque apartment fortress by eleven-thirty. A doorman took the car. I grabbed her hand and brought her to a nice proximity.

"There are people watching!" she objected. Not too strenuously.

"It's New York. Nobody gives a shit."

We kissed. And true to my prediction, no one in the city gave a damn. But us.

"Let's meet for lunch," I said.

"It's lunchtime *now*."

"That's great. We're right on time."

"I have a job to go to," Marcie said.

"No sweat—I'm cozy with your boss."

"But you have obligations. Who was guarding civil liberties while you were out of town?"

Hah. She wouldn't hoist me by my previous petard.

"Marcie, I'm here to exercise my fundamental right to the pursuit of happiness."

"Not in the street."

"We'll go upstairs and have . . . a cup of Ovaltine."

"Mr. Barrett, go directly to your goddamn office, do legalizing or whatever, and come back for dinner."

"When?" I asked impatiently.

"At dinnertime," she said, and tried to move inside. But I still held her hand.

"I'm hungry now."

"You'll have to wait till nine."

"Six-thirty," I retorted.

"Half past eight," she counteroffered.

"Seven," I insisted.

"Eight o'clock's the bottom line."

"You drive a ruthless bargain," I responded, acquiescing.

"I'm a ruthless bitch," she said. Then smiled and sprinted through the iron gates of her enormous castle.

In the office elevator, I began to yawn. Our shut-eye had been minimal and only now were the effects affecting me. I also looked exactly like a human wrinkle. At one of our coffee stops, I'd bought a cheapo razor and attempted shaving. No machines, however, were dispensing shirts. So I inevitably looked like I'd been doing what I had been doing.

"Well, it's Mr. Romeo!" Anita cried.

Who the hell had told her?

"It says right on your sweater: 'Alfa Romeo.' I thought it was your name. You surely aren't Mr. Barrett. He is always in the office with the dawn."

"I overslept," I said, and started for the refuge of my chamber.

"Oliver, get ready for a shock."

I paused.

"What happened?"

"Flower people have attacked."

"What?"

"Can't you smell from here?"

I entered what was once my office and was now a huge botanical extravaganza. Floral effervescence everywhere. Even my own desk was now . . . a bed of roses.

"Somebody loves you," said Anita, sniffing sweetly at the door.

"Was there a card?" I queried, praying that she hadn't opened it.

"On your roses—I mean on your desk," she said.

I reached for it. Thank heaven it was sealed and indicated "Personal."

"It's very heavy paper," said Anita. "When I held it to the light I couldn't read a thing."

"You can go to lunch," I answered, giving her a non-caloric smile.

"What's happened, Oliver?" she said while scrutinizing me. (My shirt was slightly frazzled, but no other clues. I'd checked.)

"What do you mean, Anita?"

"You neglected totally to hassle me for messages."

I told her once again to go and snicker out at lunch. And hang "Do not disturb" out on the knob.

"Who has that kind of signs? This isn't a motel, y'know!" She left and shut the door.

I nearly ripped the envelope to shreds while opening. The message was:

> I didn't know your favorite
> and didn't want to disappoint.
> Love,
> M.

I smiled and grabbed the phone.

"She's in conference. May I say who's calling?"

"It's her Uncle Abner," I said, sounding as avuncular as possible. There was a pause, a click, and suddenly the boss.

"Yes?"

Marcie on the line, her tone extremely crisp.

"How come your tone's so goddamn crisp?"

"I'm in a meeting with the West Coast managers."

Aha, the upper echelon. The varsity. And she was giving them her imitation of a Frigidaire.

"I'll call you back," said Marcie, clearly desperate to preserve her frosty image.

"I'll just be brief," I said. "The flowers were a lovely touch—"

"That's fine," she answered. "I'll get back to you—"

"And one more thing. You've got the most fantastic ass—"

A sudden click. The bitch hung up on me!

My heart ached and a drowsy numbness filled my soul.

"Is he dead?"

Vaguely I began to comprehend more words on the horizon of my consciousness. The voice resembled that of Barry Pollack, a recent law grad who'd just joined the firm.

"He looked so healthy just this morning."

Now Anita, trying for an Oscar as bereaved relation.

"How did he get there?" Barry asked.

I sat up. Christ, I had been sleeping on my bed of roses!

"Hi, guys," I murmured, yawning but pretending that I always took siestas on my desk. "Try knocking next time, huh?"

"We did," said Barry nervously, "a lot of times. So then we opened up to see if you were . . . uh—y'know—all right."

"I'm fine," I answered, nonchalantly flicking petals from my shirt.

"I'll make you coffee," said Anita, exiting.

"What's up, Barry?" I inquired.

"Uh . . . the—you know—School Board case. We're—you know—prepping it together."

"Yeah," I said, as it began to dawn on me that in another world I used to be a lawyer. "Don't we have a meeting on it sometime?"

"Yeah. Today at three," said Barry, shuffling papers, shifting from his right foot to his left.

"Okay, see you then."

"Uh . . . it's sort of half past four," said Barry, hoping earnestly that accuracy would not cause offense.

"Four-thirty? Holy shit!" I leapt onto my feet.

"I've got a lot of research—" Barry started, thinking that the session had begun.

"No. Hey, Barry—look, let's meet tomorrow on it, huh?" I headed for the door.

"What time?"

"You name it—first thing in the morning."

"Half past eight?"

I paused. The School Board case was actually not quite the first thing I had planned for my matutinal activities.

"No. I'm seeing . . . an executive. We'd better make it ten."

"Okay."

"Ten-thirty would be better, Bar."

"Okay."

As I burst out the door, I heard him mutter, "I've done really lots of research. . . ."

I was early for the doctor, but was glad to leave. London wasn't on my wavelength, and besides, there were momentous things to do. Like get a haircut. And select my wardrobe. Should I wear a tie?

And bring a toothbrush?

Shit, I still had hours more to wait. And so I ran in Central Park to pass the time.

And also pass her house.

The castle of the princess is protected by a regiment. At first you meet the Keeper of the Gate, who vigorously questions the legitimacy of your presence in the royal precinct. Then, if satisfied, he will direct you to an antechamber where a footman by a switchboard then attempts to verify if you, a humble commoner, are actually expected by the monarchy.

"Yes, Mr. Barrett," said the epauletted Cerberus, "you may go in." His implication was that—to his mind—I'd barely passed.

"That's splendid news," I answered him in kind. "Can you direct me to the Binnendale apartment?"

"Cross the courtyard, take the far right entrance, then the elevator to the top."

"What's the number?" I inquired.

"There's only one apartment, Mr. Barrett."

"Thanks. I'm ever so obliged" (you pompous asshole).

There was no number on the single door. Nor any indication whatsoever of who dwelt therein. As I clutched my small bouquet of flowers purchased on the corner, I rang very couthly.

Seconds later, Marcie opened. She wore a kind of silky thing that women wear around the house—if they're the Queen of Sheba. Anyway, I liked the parts the garment didn't cover.

"Hey, you look familiar," Marcie said.

"I intend to act much more so when I get inside," I answered.

"Why wait?"

I didn't. And I ran my hands on lots of silky-covered Marcie. Then I offered her the flowers.

"That's all I could scrounge up," I said. "Some lunatic bought up all the others in the city."

Marcie took my arm and led me in.

And in and in.

The place was so enormous it was disconcerting. Even though the furnishings were all in perfect taste, there just was too damn much of everything. But mostly a preponderance of space.

On the walls were many of the selfsame artworks that had graced my dorm at Harvard. Though of course these weren't reproductions.

"I like your interesting museum," I remarked.

"I liked your fascinating phone call," she retorted, deftly dodging all responsibility for ostentation.

Suddenly we found ourselves inside a coliseum.

I suppose the area was commonly referred to as a living room, but it was truly mammoth. Ceilings twenty feet at least. Huge windows overlooking Central Park. The view distracted me from adequate appraisal of the paintings. Though some, I noted, were surrealistic. Likewise their effect on me.

Marcie was amused that I was acting fazed.

"It's tiny, but it's home," she quipped.

"Jesus, Marcie, you could set a tennis court up right in here."

"I would," she answered, "if you'd play with me."

It was taking quite a while just to traverse this wide expanse. Our footsteps clicked in stereo upon the parquet floor.

"Where we going?" I inquired. "Pennsylvania?"

"Somewhere cozier," she said. And squeezed my arm.

Some moments later we were in the library. A fireplace was glowing. And our drinks were waiting.

"A toast?" she asked.

"To Marcie's ass," I said, my goblet in the air.

"No," Marcie disapproved.

I then proposed, "To Marcie's tits."

"Come on," she vetoed.

"All right, to Marcie's mind—"

"That's better."

"—as full of loveliness as Marcie's tits and ass."

"You're crude," she said.

"I'm awfully sorry," I apologized profoundly. "I will henceforth totally desist."

"Please, Oliver," she said, "do *not*. I love it."

And so we drank to that.

Several glasses later, I was loose enough to comment on the nature of her homestead.

"Hey, Marcie, how can someone who's alive as you stand living in a mausoleum? I mean my family house was *big*, but I had lawns to play on. All you have is rooms. Ancient musty rooms."

She shrugged.

"Where did you and Michael live?" I asked.

"A duplex on Park Avenue."

"Which he now owns?"

She nodded yes, then adding, "Though I got my track shoes back."

"Very generous," I said, "but then you moved back in with Daddy?"

"Sorry, Doctor, I am not *that* freaky. After the divorce, my father wisely sent me on a tour of duty to the distant branches. And I worked like hell. It was a kind of therapy-apprenticeship. He died suddenly. I came back for the funeral and stayed here. Temporarily, I told myself. I knew I should've closed the house. But since each morning I was sitting at what used to be my father's desk, some atavistic reflex made me feel I had to come . . . back home."

"Be it ever so unhumble," I appended. Then I rose, went over to her chair and placed my hand upon a lovely part of her anatomy.

No sooner had I touched her than a ghost appeared!

At least an ancient crone dressed all in black, except for a white lace collar and an apron.

It spoke.

"I knocked," it said.

"Yes, Mildred?" Marcie answered casually, as I attempted to retract my fingers up my sleeve.

"Dinner's ready," said the beldam, and evaporated. Marcie smiled at me.

And I smiled back.

For despite the odd surroundings, I was strangely happy. If for no other reason than the nearness of . . . another individual. I'd forgotten what the mere proximity to someone else's heartbeat could evoke.

"Are you hungry, Oliver?"

"I'm sure I will be by the time we reach the cafeteria." And so we went. Down yet another gallery, across the soon-to-be-constructed tennis court, to the mahogany-and-crystal dining room.

"Lest you be misled," said Marcie as we sat at the enormous table, "dinner was designed by me, but executed by a surrogate."

"You mean a cook."

"I do. I'm not domestic, Oliver."

"Marcie, have no fear. My recent diet has been more or less like Alpo dog food."

Dinner was unlike the night before in every way.

The food, of course, was better, but the conversation infinitely worse.

"Gee, delicious vichyssoise . . . beef Wellington . . . ah, Château Margaux fifty-nine . . . this soufflé is fantastic."

So much for my effusions. Otherwise I simply ate.

"Oliver, you seem a little quiet."

"I'm just speechless at these gastronomic wonders," I replied. She sensed my irony.

"I overdid it, huh?" she said.

"Marce, you didn't have to make a fuss. I don't care *what* we eat. It only matters that we're eating with each other."

"Yes," she said.

But I could see she thought that I was criticizing her. I guess I was. But not intending to cause any grief. I hoped I hadn't made her feel upset.

Anyway, I tried to reassure her.

"Hey—it doesn't mean that I don't like this, Marcie. Really. It reminds me of my home."

"Which you despised."

"Who said so?"

"You did. Yesterday."

"Oh, yeah."

I guess I'd let it all hang out at HoJo's. (Was it only one short day ago?)

"Hey, look," I said. "I'm sorry if you were offended. Somehow when my parents eat like this, it seems arthritic. On the other hand, with you it's . . . elegant."

"Do you really think so?"

This one called for some diplomacy.

"No," I said, sincerely.

"My feelings aren't hurt," she said, her feelings obviously hurt. "I wanted to impress you. I don't eat this way too often."

That was a relief to learn.

"Well, how often?"

"Twice," she said.

"A week?"

"Twice since Father died." (Which was six years ago.)

I felt bastardly for asking.

"Shall we have coffee elsewhere?" asked the hostess.

"Can I pick the room?" I asked, abrim with innuendo.

"No," said Marcie. "In my bailiwick you follow me."

I did. Back to the library. Where coffee waited and some hidden speakers wafted Mozart.

"Have you really only entertained here twice?" I asked.

She nodded yes. "Both times for business."

"How about your social life?" I asked, attempting to be delicate.

"It's gotten better lately," she replied.

"No, seriously, Marce, what would you normally do upon a New York evening?"

"Well," she said, "it's truly fascinating. I come home and jog if it's still light outside. Then back to work. My office here has got extensions from the switchboard, so I take the California calls. . . ."

"Till after twelve, I'll bet."

"Not always."

"Then what happens afterward?"

"I stop and socialize."

"Aha. Which means . . . ?"

"Oh, ginger ale and sandwiches with Johnny."

"Johnny?" (I'm incapable of masking jealousy.)

"Carson. He makes witty dinner conversation."

"Oh," I said. Relieved, I shifted back to offense.

"Don't you do anything but work?"

"Marshall McLuhan says, 'Where the whole man is involved there is no work.' "

"He's full of shit and so are you. No, Marce. You tell yourself you're so involved, but actually you're just attempting to make 'work' anesthetize your loneliness."

"Jesus, Oliver," she said, somewhat surprised. "How can you know so much about a person that you've barely met?"

"I can't," I answered. "I was talking of myself."

Curious. We both knew what we wanted next, yet neither dared disrupt the conversation. Finally, I had to broach some trivial realities.

"Hey, Marcie, it's eleven-thirty."

"Do you have a curfew, Oliver?"

"Oh, no. I also don't have other things. Like clothes, for instance."

"Was I coy or vague?" she asked.

"Let's say you weren't crystal clear," I said, "and I was not about to show up with my little canvas overnight bag."

Marcie smiled.

"That was deliberate," she confessed.

"Why?"

She stood and offered me her hand.

Across the bed were strewn no fewer than a dozen shirts of silk. My size.

"Suppose I want to stay a year?" I asked.

"This may sound somewhat odd, my friend, but if you've got the inclination, I've got all the shirts."

"Marcie?"

"Yes?"

"I've got a lot of . . . inclination."

Then we made love as if the night before had only been the dress rehearsal.

Morning came too soon. It seemed like only 5 A.M. and yet the buzzer from the clock on Marcie's side was sounding reveille.

"What time is?" I snorted.

"Five A.M.," said Marcie. "Rise and shine." She kissed my forehead.

"Are you berserk?"

"You know the court's reserved for six."

"Come on, no court's in session—" Then I wakened to her meaning. "You have *tennis* planned?"

"It's booked from six to eight. Seems a shame to waste it. . . ."

"Hey, I've got a better notion of what we could do."

"What?" Marcie ingénued, though I had started touching her already. "Volleyball?"

"Yes, if that's what you would like to call it."

Anyway, whatever it was called, she was amenable to playing.

The difference was the bathroom.

As I showered, I was meditating on what elements distinguished Walter Binnendale's abode from Dover House, my parents' joint in Ipswich, Massachusetts.

Not the art. For *we* had masterpieces too. Although, befitting our more ancient fortune, of a prior century. The furnishings were vaguely similar. To me antique means old; I don't appreciate the vintages of bric-a-brac.

But the bathrooms! Here the Barretts proved themselves inextricably bound to Puritan tradition: rooms functional and basic. White-tile, simple—Spartan, one might even say. Surely nothing one might *linger* in. But not the Binnendales. *Their* baths were worthy of a Roman emperor. Or more precisely of the modern Roman *principe* who had created them. The mere notion of "designing" such a room would have outraged the liberalest of Barretts.

In the mirror through the slightly opened portal I could see the bedroom.

Where a wagon entered.

Pushed by Mildred.

Cargo: breakfast.

By the time I'd wiped my face off, Marcie was at table—in a garment she did not intend to wear to work (I hope). I sat down clad in merely towel.

"Coffee, bacon, eggs?"

"Jesus, it's a damn hotel!"

"Are you *still* complaining, Mr. Barrett?"

"No, it was fun," I answered, buttering a muffin, "and I'd like to come again 'cause it was silly." Then I paused. And told her, "In, like, thirty years."

She looked perplexed.

"Marce," I said, "this place is strictly for the paleologists. It's full of sleeping dinosaurs."

She looked at me.

"This isn't what you really want," I said.

Her face seemed sort of moved.

"I want to be with you," she answered.

She wasn't coy. Or full of metaphor, as I had been.

"Okay," I said. To give me time to think of what to say.

"When would you like to go?" she asked.

"Today," I answered.

Marcie wasn't fazed.

"Just tell me when and where."

"Let's meet at five o'clock in Central Park. The East Side entrance to the reservoir."

"What should I bring?" she asked.

"Your track shoes," I replied.

I fell thirty thousand feet and hit the ground. I was incredibly depressed.

"It's unbearable," I told the doctor. "Couldn't you have warned me?"

Earlier that afternoon, my wild euphoria had started to dissolve into a sadness beyond words.

"But nothing's wrong—" I started. Then I realized how ridiculous it sounded. "I mean things are going well with Marcie. It's just me. I've clutched. I can't go through with it."

There was a pause. I hadn't specified what I could not go through with.

I knew. But it was difficult to say:

"Taking her to my place. Do you understand?"

Once again I'd acted rashly. Why the haste in making Marcie leave her house? Why do I precipitate these gestures of . . . commitment?

"Maybe I'm just using Marcie selfishly . . . to fill the void." I thought about my own hypothesis.

"Or maybe it's still Jenny. I mean almost two years later I could maybe have a fling and justify it. But my *house!* To have somebody in my house and in my bed. Sure, realistically the house is different and the bed is different. Logic says it shouldn't bother me. But damn, it *does.*"

"Home," you see, is still a place I live with Jenny.

Paradox: They say that husbands all have fantasies of being single. I'm a weirdo. I lapse into daydreams that I'm married.

And it helps to have a place that is inviolate. A pad that no one comes to. I mean nothing breaks the comforting illusion that I'm sharing all I have with someone.

Now and then a piece of mail is forwarded, addressed to both of us. And Radcliffe regularly sends her letters coaxing contributions. This is my dividend for not announcing Jenny's death except to friends.

The only other toothbrush in the bathroom has belonged to Philip Cavilleri.

So you see, it's either a dishonest act to one girl . . .

Or betrayal of another.

Dr. London spoke.

"In either case, that puts you in the wrong."

He understood. But unexpectedly his understanding made it even worse.

"Must it be only either/or?" he queried with a Kierkegaardian allusion. "Could there be no other explanation for your conflict?"

"What?" I really didn't know.

A pause.

"You like her," Dr. London quietly suggested.

I considered it.

"Which one?" I asked. "You didn't say a name."

23

Marcie had to be postponed.

By a strange coincidence I'd set our rendezvous for 5 P.M. Which happened, as I realized in the office, to conflict directly with my psychiatric session. So I called to make adjustments.

"What's the matter—chickening, my friend?" This time there was no meeting in her office. She could tease me.

"I'll only be an hour late. Sixty minutes."

"Can I trust you?" Marcie asked.

"That's your problem, isn't it?"

Anyway, we had to run in semidarkness. Which can be lovely when the reservoir reflects the city lights.

Seeing her again, I felt some day-long qualms diminish. She was beautiful. I had forgotten quite how much. We kissed and then began to jog.

"How was your day?" I asked.

"Oh, the usual catastrophes, the overstock positions, understock positions, minor transportation snag, suicidal panic in the corridors. But mostly thoughts of you."

I fabricated things to say a stride ahead of saying them. And yet, incapable of superficial running conversation, I inevitably focused on the point. I had demanded. She had come. We both were here. What was she feeling?

"Did you wonder where we would be going?"

"I thought you had the compass, friend."

"Bring any clothes?"

"We can't eat dinner in our track suits, can we?"

I was curious to know how much she'd packed.

"Where's your stuff?"

"My car." She gestured toward Fifth Avenue. "Just an airline bag. The kind you carry on and carry off. It's very practical."

"For quick departures."

"Right," she said, pretending not to know what I was thinking. We ran another lap.

"I thought we'd go to my place," I said casually.

"Okay."

"It isn't very big . . ."

"That's fine."

". . . and just make dinner. By ourselves. The staff is you and me. I'll do the goddamn dishes. . . ."

"Fine," she answered. When we'd jogged another hundred yards, she interrupted our athletic reverie.

"But, Oliver," she said, a trifle plaintively, "who'll do the goddamn cooking?"

I looked at her.

"Something in my stomach says you aren't being jocular."

She wasn't. On our final lap she told me of her culinary training. It was nil. She once had wanted to enroll in Cordon Bleu, but Mike objected. One can always get the teacher to come cook for one. I was sort of pleased. I had mastered pasta, scrambled eggs and half a dozen other tricky dishes. This made me the expert who could introduce her to the kitchen.

On the way to my place—which takes longer if you drive than if you jog—we stopped for take-out Chinese food. I had enormous difficulty finalizing my selection.

"Problems?" Marcie asked, observing my exhaustive study of the menu.

"Yeah. I can't make up my mind."

"It's only dinner," Marcie said. And what she may have meant —or understood—I'll never know.

I am sitting in my living room, trying to read last week's Sunday *Times* and pretending that a lady in my bathroom showering is nothing extraordinary.

"Hey," I heard her call, "the towels here are sort of . . . rancid."

"Yes," I said.

"Do you have clean ones?"

"No," I said.

There was a pause.

"I'll be okay," she said.

The bathroom was suffused with smells of femininity. I thought my shower would be quick (I only had one lousy nozzle, after all), and yet the perfume made me stay. Or was I afraid to leave the reassuring flow of warmth?

I was emotional, all right. And hypersensitive. But strange to say, at this point in the evening with a woman out there waiting to play house with me according to my oddball rules, I couldn't tell if I was happy or if I was sad.

I only knew that I was feeling.

Marcie Binnendale was in the kitchenette, pretending she could light a stove.

"You need *matches*, Marce," I coughed, while quickly opening the window. "I'll show you."

"Sorry, friend," she said, extremely ill at ease. "I'm lost in here."

I warmed the Chinese food, took out some beer and poured an orange juice. Marcie set the (coffee) table.

"Where'd you get these knives and forks?" she asked.

"Oh, here and there."

"I'll say. No two pieces match."

"I like variety." (Yes. We had owned a total set. It's stashed away with other stuff suggesting marriage.)

We sat down on the floor and had our dinner. I was as loose as my uptightness would allow. I wondered if the grunge of the apartment and its claustrophobic clutter made my guest nostalgic for her normal way of life.

"It's nice," she said. And touched my hand. "Do you have any music?"

"No." (I'd given Jenny's stereo away.)

"Nothing?"

"Just the radio that wakes me up."

"Okay if I tune in to QXR?" she asked.

I nodded, tried to smile, and Marcie rose. The radio was by the bed. Which was some four or five steps' journey from where we were camping. I was wondering if she'd return or wait for me to join her there. Could she notice my depression? Did she think my ardor had already waned?

Suddenly the telephone.

Marcie stood above it.

"Shall I answer, Oliver?"

"Why not?"

"It could be some little friend of yours," she smiled.

"You flatter me. Impossible. You answer it."

She shrugged and did.

"Good evening. . . . Yes, that number is correct. . . . It is. He's . . . Who am I? How is that relevant?"

Who the hell was at the other end, interrogating my own private guests? I rose and sternly grabbed the phone.

"Yeah? Who is this?"

A silence on the other end was broken by a gravelly "Congratulations!"

"Oh—Phil."

"Well, glory be to God," the holy Cavilleri rolled.

"How are you, Phil?" I said casually.

He totally ignored my question while pursuing his.

"Is she nice?"

"Who, Philip?" I retorted icily.

"Her, the she, the gal who answered."

"Oh, that's just the maid," I said.

"At ten o'clock at night? Come on—come off it. Level with me."

"I mean my secretary. You recall Anita—with the lots of hair. I'm giving her some notes about my School Board case."

"Don't bullshit me. If that's Anita, I'm the Cardinal of Cranston."

"Phil, I'm busy."

"Sure, I know. And I'll hang up. But don't tell me you're gonna write no letters when I do."

Philip, never one to talk in whispers, had been responding at a pitch so loud it broadcast through the whole apartment. Marcie was amused.

"Hey," I inquired, so coolly I impressed myself, "when will we get together?"

"At the weddin'," Philip said.

"Whaat?"

"Hey, is she tall or small? Or fat or thin? Or light or dark?"

"She's pumpernickel."

"Ah," said Phil, and pounced upon my jocular detail, "you do admit that she's a she. Now, does she like you?"

"I don't know."

"Ignore the question. Sure she likes you. You're terrific. If she needs some selling, I'll just pep her on the phone. Hey—put her on."

"Don't bother."

"Then she's sold? She digs you?"

"I don't know."

"Then what's she doin' in your house at ten P.M.?"

Tears of laughter poured down Marcie's face. At *me*. Because I was so bad at playing Puritan.

"Oliver, I know I'm interruptin', so I'll ask you one quick question and the ball is yours to do with as your heart contents."

"About our meeting, Phil—"

"Oliver, that's not my question."

"What's your question, Philip?"

"When's the weddin', Oliver?"

He hung up loudly. I could sense his laughter all the way from Cranston.

"Who was that?" asked Marcie, though I'm sure she guessed. "He seems to love you very much."

I looked at her with gratitude for understanding.

"Yeah. The feeling's mutual."

Marcie came and sat upon the bed. And took my hand.

"I know you feel uncomfortable," she said.

"It's sort of crowded here," I answered.

"In your head as well. And mine." We sat in silence. How much had she intuited?

"I never slept with Michael in the big apartment," Marcie offered.

"I never slept with Jenny . . . here."

"I understand," she said. "But if I met his parents it would just evoke a headache or a touch of nausea. Anything that brings up Jenny is still agony for you."

I could not refute a single thing she said.

"Should I go home?" she asked. "I'd really understand if you said yes."

Without the slightest introspection—for it was the *only* way—I answered no.

"Let's take a walk. And have a drink outside."

Marcie had this strange take-over manner. I mean I liked her strength. And her ability to . . . cope with situations.

Wine for me and orange juice for her.

She sensed I wanted to hang in there, so she kept the conversation superficial. We discussed her occupation.

Not many of us know exactly what the presidents of chain stores *do*. It's not that glamorous. They have to visit every store and walk down every single aisle.

"How often?"

"All the time. When I'm not doing that, I check the shows in

Europe and the Orient. To get a feel of what the next big sexy thing might be."

"What is 'sexy' in the business connotation, Marce?"

"When you wear that stupid cashmere thing I gave you, you promote our 'fantasy' or 'sexy' line. Look, twenty different stores can sell a simple sweater. But we're always on the prowl for image-makers, items people never knew they needed. If we're right, they see it in our ad and kill each other to be first in line. You dig?"

"In economic terms," I said with Ivy League pomposity, "you build a false demand for a supply of what inherently is worthless."

"Dull but accurate." She nodded.

"Put in brighter terms, if you say, 'Shit is in,' then everybody buys manure."

"Correct. Our only problem is if someone gets that brilliant notion first!"

Marcie's car was parked (illegally) in front of my apartment. It was late when we got back. But I felt better. Or the wine had made me think I did.

"Well," she said, "I've walked you home."

Exquisite tact. I had both options now. I also knew which one I . . . needed.

"Marcie, if you go, you'll sleep alone and I'll sleep alone. In economic terms, that's inefficient use of bedroom space. Would you agree?"

"I would," she said.

"Besides, I'd really like to put my arms around you."

She acknowledged a coincidental inclination.

Marcie woke me with a cup of coffee.

In a Styrofoam container?

"I couldn't start the stove," she said. "I went out to the corner shop."

24

Please understand. We aren't "living together."

Although it's been a summer of excitement.

It's true we eat together, talk together, laugh (and disagree) together, sleep together under the same roof (i.e., my basement). But neither party has acknowledged an arrangement. And certainly no obligations. Everything is day-to-day. Although we try as much as possible to be with one another. We do have something rather rare, I think. A kind of . . . friendship. And it's all the more unusual because it's not platonic.

Marcie keeps her wardrobe at the castle and picks up mail and messages when she's exchanging garments. Happily, at times she also picks up food prepared by her now underactive staff. We eat it off the coffee table with disparate spoons and rap about whatever's in the air. Will LBJ stand up in history? ("Damn tall.") What horror show will Nixon stage to "Vietnamize"? Moon shots while the cities fester. Dr. Spock. James Earl Ray. Chappaquiddick. Green Bay Packers. Spiro T. Jackie O. Would the world be better if Cosell and Kissinger changed jobs?

Sometimes Marcie has to work till nearly twelve. I pick her up, we have a midnight sandwich and walk slowly home—that is, to my place.

Sometimes I'm in Washington, which means that she's alone—although there's always stuff to keep her busy. Then she meets my shuttle at La Guardia and drives me in. But mostly, I'm the one providing airport transportation.

Look, the nature of her work involves a lot of travel. The obligatory visits to each branch. Which means at least a week away while covering the Eastern corridor, part of another week for Cleveland, Cincinnati and Chicago. And of course the Western circuit: Denver, L.A., San Francisco. Naturally, the absences are not consecutive. For one, New York's the base of operations, where she has to "charge her batteries." And lately, for another, it's the place she charges mine. We have a lot of days together. Now and then we even have a week.

Naturally, I'd like to see her more, but understand what her commitments mean. The papers nowadays decry what they call sexist-male suppression of his partner's individuality. But I won't be hung with that rap twice. And I see other couples far less fortunate than we. Luci Danziger has tenure in the Princeton Psych Department and her husband, Peter, teaches math in Boston. Even double academic salaries don't allow them luxuries that Marce and I enjoy: the myriad of phone calls, stolen weekends in exotic midway places (I could write a song about our recent Cincinnati idyll).

I do confess I'm lonely when she's out of town. Especially in summer, with the lovers in the park. The telephone's a pretty meager substitute. Because the minute you hang up, your hand is empty.

We are, from what I gather in the media, a modern couple. He works. She works. They share responsibilities—or lack of them. They show respect for one another. Probably they don't want children.

Actually, I would like children someday. And I don't think marriage is so obsolete. But anyway, the whole discussion's moot. Marcie's never advocated motherhood or matrimony. She seems pleased with what we have. Which is, I guess, affection bound by neither time nor definition.

None of this is stuff we talk about when we're together. We're too busy doing things. Part of our incessant motion is the fact it keeps us out of my adobe (though Marcie's never once complained of claustrophobia). We jog. We play a lot of tennis (not at 6 A.M.; I put my sneaker down). We see a lot of movies and whatever Walter Kerr suggests is worthwhile in the theater. We share a common phobia for parties; we're jealous of each other's company and like to be alone. Still, now and then we do see friends upon a casual evening.

Rightfully, Steve Simpson claimed a moral option on our first night out. Gwen was hot to cook, but sharp dyspeptic apprehensions made me vote for Giamatti's in the Village. Okay, cool—we'll see you both at eight.

Now, Marcie has this little social problem. She's a conversation-stopper. Which isn't something teen-age girls should dream of. First, we can't ignore the matter of her looks (indeed, *that* is the essence of the problem). Take Steve—a normal, happy husband. He examines Marcie's physiognomy, albeit from afar, in manner somewhat less than nonchalant. He doesn't stare exactly, but he does indulge in rather heavy gazing. Thus, a priori, Marcie has already put off someone else's wife. And even though she dresses with consistent understatement, other females seem to ferret out the fashion. And are not too pleased.

We move across the sawdust floor of Giamatti's. Stephen is already standing (good manners, or for better viewing?). Gwen is smiling on the outside. Doubtless hoping that for all her poise and obvious panache, at least my girl will be a five-watt bulb.

Introductions are another hurdle. You say "Binnendale" and even a sophisticate is not unmoved. With most celebrities there is a built-in, solid-state reaction ("Loved your piece on boxing, Mr. Mailer"; "How's the national security, Professor Kissinger?" and so on). Always there's a point of reference you can gloss upon. But what to say to Marcie: "Liked your new displays"?

Marcie copes, of course. Her policy is always to initiate the conversation. Though she ends up doing lots of talking *at*. Which obviously makes it tough to get to know her. And which explains why people often find her cold.

Anyway, we start with badinage like Giamatti's is so tough to find. ("Did you get lost as well?") John Lennon eats here when he's in New York. The common party lines.

Then Marcie literally grabs the ball. She's very anxious to display her friendliness to friends of mine. She buckshots Steve with questions on neurology. And doing so, evinces more than layman's knowledge of the field.

On learning that Gwen teaches history at Dalton, she dilates on the state of New York City's private education. Back in her day at Brearley, things were pretty rigid, structured, all the rest. She speaks enthusiastically about the innovations. Especially the mathematics programs, training kids to use computers when they're very young.

Gwen has vaguely heard about this stuff. Of course with all the hours of history she teaches, there's no time to get the feedback from the other disciplines. Yet she observes how Marcie's so well tuned in to the current New York academic scene. Marcie answers that she reads lots of magazines on planes.

Anyway, I cringe at much of this. And hurt for Marcie. No one ever gets to glimpse the ugly duckling underneath the outer swan. They can't conceive she's so unconfident she comes on extra strong to compensate. I understand. But I'm no good at chairing conversations.

Anyway, I try. And turn to topics in the world of sport. Steve is warmed and Gwen relieved. Very soon we're ranging far and wide on jocky issues of the day—the Stanley Cup, the Davis Cup, Phil Esposito, Derek Sanderson, Bill Russell, will the Yankees move to Jersey—and I'm having too much fun to notice anything except the ice is broken. Everybody's loose. We're even using locker-room locutions.

Only when the waiter takes the order do I notice that the song has only been a trio. When I hear Gwen Simpson join the conversation, saying, "I'll have the *scaloppine alla minorese.*"

"What the hell is wrong with Marcie?"

Thus Steve to me a few days later as we finished jogging. (This was Marcie's week to walk the Eastern corridor.) I'd asked him casually, to get some notion of what he and Gwen had thought. As we left the park and crossed Fifth Avenue, he asked again, "What's wrong with her?"

"What do you mean—'What's wrong with her?' There's *nothing* wrong, goddammit."

Stephen looked at me and shook his head. I had not understood.

"That's just the point," he said. "She's goddamn perfect."

What the hell is wrong with me?

I've just been readmitted to the human race. The petals of my soul are opening. I should be overjoyed. And yet for some strange reason, I feel only mezzo-mezzo. Maybe it's just leaves-are-falling blues.

Not that I'm depressed.

How could I be? I'm cooking on all burners. Working well. So much so I can now devote more hours to the Raiders up in Harlem and to civil liberties.

As for Marcie, in the words of Stephen Simpson, it is goddamn perfect. Our interests coincide in almost everything.

And we are literally a team. Mixed doubles, to be quite specific. Competing in a tourney for the tristate area. We conquered Gotham Club with ease and have been facing combos from the provinces. With moderate success (which is to say we're undefeated).

She deserves the credit. I'm outclassed by more than half the guys, but Marcie simply runs the legs off all her female competition. I never thought I'd see myself admit athletic mediocrity. But I just hang in there, and thanks to Marcie, we've won ribbons and certificates, and are en route to our first gold-leaf trophy.

And she's been really Marcie-like as we advance in competition. Being victims of the schedule, we have to play on certain nights—or forfeit. Once the Gotham quarter final was a Wednesday 9 P.M. She'd spent the day in Cleveland, took a dinner flight, put on her tennis clothes before they landed, and while I was bullshitting the referee, appeared by nine-fifteen. We edged a victory, went home and crashed. Next morning she was off again at seven to Chicago. Happily, there was no game the week she spent out on the Coast.

To sum it up: a man and woman synchronized in mood and pace of life. It *works*.

Then why the hell am I not quite as happy as the scoreboard says I should be?

Clearly this was topic number one with Dr. London.

"It's not depression, Doctor. I feel great. I'm full of optimism. Marce and I . . . the two of us . . ."

I paused. I had intended to say, "We communicate incessantly." But it is difficult to pull a fast one on yourself.

". . . we don't talk to one another."

Yes, I said it. And I meant it, though it sounded paradoxical. For did we not—as well our bills attested—gab for hours nightly on the phone?

Yes. But we don't really *say* that much.

"I'm happy, Oliver" is not communication. It is just a testimonial.

I could be wrong, of course.

What the hell do I know of relationships? All I've ever been is married. And it doesn't seem appropriate to make comparisons with Jenny. I mean, I only know the two of us were very much in love. At the time, of course, I wasn't analytical. I didn't scrutinize my feelings through a psychiatric microscope. And I can't articulate precisely why with Jenny I was so supremely happy.

Yet the funny thing is Jen and I had so much less in common. She was passionately unimpressed by sports. When I watched football she would read a book across the room.

I taught her how to swim.

I never did succeed in teaching her to drive.

But what the hell—is being man and wife some kind of educational experience?

You bet your ass it is.

But not in swimming, driving or in reading maps. Or even—as I recently had tried to recreate the situation—in teaching someone how to light a stove.

It means you learn about yourself from constant dialogue with one another. Establishing new circuits in the satellite transmitting your emotions.

Jenny would have nightmares and would wake me up. In those days, before we knew how sick she was, she'd ask me, genuinely scared, "If I can't have a baby, Oliver—would you still feel the same?"

Which didn't prompt a knee-jerk reassurance on my part. Instead, it opened up a whole new complex of emotions that I hadn't known were there. Yes, Jen, it would upset my ego not to have a baby born of you, the person that I love.

This didn't alter our relationship. Instead, her honest qualm provoking such an honest question made me realize that I wasn't such a hero. That I wasn't really ready to face childlessness with great maturity and big bravado. I told her I would need some help from *her*. And then we knew ourselves a whole lot better, thanks to our admissions of self-doubt.

And we were closer.

"Jesus, Oliver, you didn't bullshit."

"Did the unheroic truth upset you, Jenny?"

"No, I'm glad."

"How come?"

"Because I know you never bullshit, Oliver."

Marce and I don't have that kind of conversation yet. I mean, she tells me when she's down and when she's nervous. And that she worries sometimes when she's on the road that I might find a new "diversion." Actually, that feeling's mutual. Yet strangely, when we talk we say the proper words, but they trip out too easily upon the tongue.

Maybe that's because I have exaggerated expectations. I'm impatient. People who have had a happy marriage know exactly what they need. And lack. But it's unfair to make precipitous demands of someone who has never had a . . . friend . . . that she could trust.

Still, I'm hoping someday she will *need* me more. That she will maybe even wake me up and ask me something like:

"If I can't have a baby, would you feel the same?"

"Marcie, I may cry a lot this week."

It was 6 A.M. and we were standing at the airport.

"Eleven days," she said. "The longest that we've been apart."

"Yeah," I said, and smiled. "But I was thinking I just might receive a dose of tear gas at the demonstration."

"You act like you're looking forward to it, Oliver."

Touché. To catch a little gas is kind of macho in some circles. She had caught me with my ego down.

"And also don't provoke a goddamn cop," she added.

"I promise. I'll behave."

They called her flight. A fleeting kiss and then I trotted—yawning—to get on the shuttle down to Washington.

I candidly confess. I like it when Important Causes ask my help. This Saturday was New Mobe's huge November End-the-War parade in Washington. Three days earlier, the organizers called me to come down and help negotiate with all the boys in Justice. "We really need your bod," said Freddie Gardner. I was peacock proud until they told me that it wasn't only for my legal expertise but "'cause you cut your hair and look like a Republican."

The issue was what route the march would take. Traditionally, parades in Washington go right down Pennsylvania Avenue and by the Presidential Palace. Squads of government attorneys argued this one had to be more *south*. (How far? I thought. The Panama Canal?)

Marcie got a blow-by-blow each night.

"Kleindienst kept insisting, 'There'll be violence, there'll be violence.'"

"How the hell did he know?" Marcie asked.

"That's just the point. I asked him, 'How the fuck do you know?'"

"You employed those words?"

"Well . . . all but one. In any case he answered, 'Mitchell says so.'"

"How the hell does Mitchell know?"

"I asked. He wouldn't answer. I had the sudden urge to throw a punch."

"Oh, that's mature. Are you behaving, Oliver?"

"If sexy thoughts were crimes, then I'd get life."

"I'm glad," she said.

Our phone bills were phenomenal.

Thursday afternoon two bishops and a pride of priests arranged a Mass for Peace outside the Pentagon. We were forewarned that they would be arrested, so we had a congregation packed with lawyers.

"Was there any violence?" Marcie asked that evening.

"No. The cops were really courteous. But man, the crowd! It was incredible. They shouted things at priests they wouldn't shout in drunken bars! Christ, I wanted to throw punches."

"Did you?"

"Mentally."

"That's good."

"I miss you, Marce. I'd like to get my hands on you."

"Keep that inside your head as well. What happened to the priests?"

"We had to go to court in Alexandria to help the bailing out. It went okay. Why did you change the goddamn subject? Can't I say I miss you?"

By Friday, the administration had revenge. Doubtless through the prayers of Mr. Nixon (via Billy Graham), Washington was throttled by a cold wet chill. And yet it didn't stop the candle-light procession, headed by Bill Coffin, Yale's amazing chaplain. Damn, that guy's enough to bring me to religion. And in fact I went to hear him later in the National Cathedral. I just stood in back (the place was mobbed) and kind of breathed the solidarity. And would've given anything for Marcie's hand to hold.

As I was making my unprecedented visit to a house of God, in Du Pont Circle hordes of Yippies, Crazies, Weathermen and other mindless assholes staged a nasty riot. Thereby giving credibility to everything I'd been denying all week long.

"Those bastards!" I told Marcie on the phone. "They aren't even *for* a cause—except self-advertisement."

"Those are the guys you should have punched," she said.

"You're goddamn right," I said with disappointment.

"Where were you?"

"In church," I said.

In rather rainbowed language Marcie indicated disbelief. Then I quoted Coffin's sermon and convinced her.

"Hey, you know," she said, "tomorrow's papers will have half a column on the service and three pages on the riot."

Sadly, she was right.

I had trouble sleeping. I felt guilty that while I was in the poshness of my cheap motel, so many thousand marchers were encamping on cold floors and benches.

Saturday was chill and windy, but at least the rain had stopped. Having no one to bail out or anything to argue for, I wandered over to St. Mark's, which was a rendezvousing place for everyone.

The church was filled with people bunking out, or having coffee, or just sitting silently to wait the cue. Everything had been well organized, with marshals to keep marchers from the cops (and vice versa). There were medicos to handle unexpected crises. Here and there I even saw a person over thirty.

By the coffee urn, some doctors were explaining to a group of volunteers how to react should tear gas manifest itself.

Sometimes when you're lonely, you imagine that you see a face you know. One female doctor looked extremely like . . . Joanna Stein.

"Hello," she said, as I was pouring coffee. It *was* Joanna.

"Don't let me interrupt the first-aid seminar."

"That's okay," she said. "I'm glad to see you here. How are you?"

"Cold," I said.

I wondered if I should apologize for never having called her back. It didn't seem the moment. Though I think her gentle face was asking.

"You look tired, Jo," I said.

"We drove all night."

"That's rough," I said, and offered her a swig of coffee.

"Are you by yourself?" she asked.

What was her implication?

"I hope I'll be with half a million others," I replied. And thought I'd covered every loophole.

"Yeah," she said.

A pause.

"Uh, by the way, Jo, how's your family?"

"My brothers are down here somewhere. Mom and Dad are stuck in New York, playing."

Then she added, "Are you marching with a group?"

"Oh, sure," I said, as casually as possible. And instantly regretted lying. For I knew she'd have invited me to join her friends.

"You're . . . looking well," Jo said to me. And I could tell that she was marking time in hopes that I might show more interest.

But I felt embarrassed simply standing there and trying to chat superficially.

"I'm sorry, Jo," I said. "I've got some buddies waiting for me in the cold. . . ."

"Oh, sure," she said. "Don't let me keep you."

"No—it's just . . ."

She saw I was uneasy and she let me go.

"Enjoy yourself."

I hesitated, then I started to go off.

"Remember me to all the music freaks," I called.

"They'd love to see you, Oliver. Come any Sunday."

Now I was some distance from her. Casually I turned and saw she'd joined another woman and two men. Clearly those she'd driven down with. Other doctors? Was one guy her boyfriend? None of your damn business, Oliver.

I marched. I didn't chant because it's not my way. Like one huge centipede we passed the District Court, the FBI and Justice, the Internal Revenue, and turned just at the Treasury. At last we reached the ithyphallic tribute to the Father of Our Country.

I froze my ass off sitting on the ground. And did a little dozing during the orations. But to me it came alive when that huge multitude joined voice and sang "Give Peace a Chance."

I didn't sing. I'm not a vocal person. Actually, if I'd been with

Joanna's group I might have. But it's strange to try a solo in a crowd.

I was pretty tired as I unlocked my New York basement door. Just then the phone began to ring. I mustered up a final sprint and grabbed it.

I was bushed enough to be light-headed.

"Hi," I squeaked falsetto. "This is Abbie Hoffman, wishing you a Yippie New Year!"

Pretty humorous, I thought.

But Marcie didn't laugh.

Because it wasn't Marcie.

"Uh—um—Oliver?"

My little joke had been a tiny bit mistimed.

"Good evening, Father. I—uh—thought you might be someone else."

"Um—yes."

A pause.

"How are you, son?"

"I'm fine. How's Mother?"

"Fine. She's here as well. Um—Oliver, about next Saturday . . ."

"Yes, sir?"

"Are we meeting in New Haven?"

I'd forgotten all about the date we'd made last June!

"Uh—sure. Of course."

"That's fine. Will you be driving?"

"Yes."

"Then shall we meet right at the Field House gate? Say, noon?"

"Okay."

"And dinner afterwards, I hope."

Come on, say yes. He wants to see you. You can hear it in his voice.

"Yes, sir."

"That's fine. Uh—Mother wants to say hello."

And thus my week of demonstration ended as I chatted undemonstratively with my parents.

Marcie called at midnight.

"The news said Nixon watched a football game while you were marching," she reported.

At this point it didn't matter.

"The goddamn house is empty," I replied.

"Just one week more . . ."

"This separation crap has got to end."

"It will, my friend. In seven days."

In my family, tradition is a substitute for love. We do not effuse affection on each other. But we instead attend the tribal functions that give testimony to our . . . allegiance. The yearly festivals are four: Christmas, Easter and Thanksgiving, naturally. And then that sacred rite of autumn, Holy Weekend. The last occasion is of course the moral Armageddon, when the Good and Evil in the world do battle, Light opposes Dark. In other words, The Game. Fair Harvard versus Yale.

It is a time to laugh and a time to weep. But most of all, it is a time to bellow, shriek, act like demented juveniles, and drink.

In my family, however, celebration is a trifle more sedate. While some alumni have their tailgate parties, lunching Bloody

Marily upon the parking fields before the clash, the Barretts take Harvardian athletics straight.

When I was a child, my father brought me to each game at Soldiers Field. He was no once-a-year man; we saw every one. His explanations were meticulous. At ten years old, I was conversant with the most exotic signals of the referees. Moreover, I learned how to cheer. My father never screamed. He'd utter, nearly to himself, "Good man," "Ah, fine," and suchlike exclamations when the Crimson acted well. And if, perchance, our gladiators weren't up to snuff, as when we lost by fifty-five to zilch, he'd comment, "Pity."

He had been an athlete, Father. Rowed for Harvard (secondarily, Olympic single sculls). He wore the honored tie with black and crimson stripes which meant he'd earned his *H*. Which also gave him the prerogative of football tickets in the best position. At the president's right hand.

Time has neither dimmed nor altered rituals of Harvard–Yale encounters. All that's changed has been my status. Rites of passage passed, I now possess an *H* myself (in hockey). I am thus entitled on my own to fifty-yard-line seats. In theory, I could bring my son and teach him how to tell a penalty for clipping.

And yet, with the exception of the years I was in college, and then married, I attend the Harvard–Yale game with my father. Mother, in the single autocratic gesture of her life, renounced the ceremony years ago. "I don't under*stand* it," she had told my father, "and my feet get cold."

When the game is held in Cambridge, we have dinner in the venerable Boston eating institution Locke-Ober's. When the battle's in New Haven, Father favors Kaysey's—less patina, better food. This year we were seated in the latter, having watched our alma mater bow by 7–0. Play had been lethargic, hence there wasn't too much football to discuss. Which left the possibility that nonathletic topics might impinge. I was determined not to speak of Marcie.

"Pity," Father said.

"It's only football," I replied, my reflex ever to take adversary stances to his points of view.

"I expected Massey to be throwing more," said Father.

"Harvard's good on pass-defense," I offered.

"Yes. Perhaps you're right."

We ordered lobster. Which takes time, especially with this huge crowd. The place was loaded to the gills with loaded Yalies. Bulldogs baying victory songs. Hymns to heroism with the pigskin. Anyway, we had a relatively quiet table and could hear each other. If indeed we had the substance of a dialogue.

"How are things?" my father asked.

"About the same," I answered. (I confess, I don't facilitate our conversations.)

"Are you . . . getting out a bit?" He tries to take an interest. I'll concede he tries.

"A bit," I said.

"That's fine," he said.

Today I sensed my father was uneasier than last year. And uneasier than he had been when we had dinner in New York before the summer.

"Oliver," he said, and in that tone which heralded portentous things, "may I be personal?"

Can he be serious?

"Of course," I said.

"I'd like to talk to you about the future."

"What about my future, sir?" I asked while inwardly dispatching my defensive unit to the field.

"Not yours exactly, Oliver. The Family's."

I had a sudden thought that he or Mother might be ill or something. They'd announce it to me in the same impassive way. Or even send a letter (Mother would).

"I'm sixty-five," he said.

"Not till March," I answered. My precision aimed to prove involvement of a sort.

"Well, nonetheless, I have to think as if I'm sixty-five already." Was my father looking forward to a social security check?

"According to the rules of partnership . . ."

But as he started, I tuned out. For I had heard a sermon from the selfsame text upon this same occasion twelve months previous. I knew the message.

Now the only difference was the post-game choreography. Last year, after several conversations with the Crimson cream, we'd headed into Boston to the favored restaurant. Father chose to park right by his State Street office, home of the sole enterprise that bore our name overtly: "Barrett, Ward and Seymour, Inc. Investment Bankers."

As we ambulated toward the eatery, Father pointed upward to the darkened windows and remarked, "It's awfully quiet in the evening, isn't it?"

"It's always quiet in your private office," I replied.

"The eye of the tornado, son."

"You like it, though."

"I do," he said. "I like it, Oliver."

Not the money, certainly. And not the naked power involved in floating giant issues for a city or utility or corporation. What he liked, I think, was the Responsibility. If the word could ever be applied to him, I'd say my father's "turn-on" was Responsibility. To the Mills that launched the Firm, the Firm itself, its Sacred Institute of Moral Guidance, Harvard. And of course, the Family.

"I'm sixty-four," my father had announced that night in Boston one whole Harvard–Yale ago.

"Next March," I'd said, consistently assuring him I knew his birthday.

". . . and according to the rules of partnership, I must retire at sixty-eight."

There was a pause. We walked the quiet Stately streets of downtown Boston.

"We should really talk about it, Oliver."

"What, sir?"

"Who follows me as senior partner . . ."

"Mr. Seymour," I suggested. After all, as both the stationery and the doors affirmed, there were two other partners.

"Seymour and his family own twelve percent," my father said, "and Ward has ten."

Let the record show I did not ask for these details.

"Aunt Helen has some token shares, which I control for her." He took a breath and said, "The rest is ours . . ."

I wanted to demur. Thus to prevent his finishing the thought.

". . . and ultimately yours."

I longed to change the subject, but was too aware of the emotional investment on my father's part. This clearly was a moment he'd prepared for with no small concern.

"Couldn't Seymour still become the senior partner?" I inquired.

"Yes. But that's if no one took . . . direct responsibility for all the Barrett interests."

"Well, suppose he did?" The implication was, suppose *I* didn't.

"Well, according to the rules of partnership, they have the option to buy out our shares." He hesitated. "But of course things wouldn't be the same."

His final phrase was not a sequitur. It was a plea.

"Sir?" I asked.

"The Family . . . involvement," Father said.

He knew I understood. He knew I knew why we had strolled so slowly. Yet the topic had exceeded walking distance. We had arrived at Locke-Ober's.

There was only time for him to add before we entered, "Think about it."

Although I nodded that I might, I knew I wouldn't think about it for a second.

Atmosphere inside was not too staid that evening. For the Crimson had wrought miracles that afternoon. The Lord had sent His wrath upon the Yalies in the final minute, through His messenger, a junior quarterback named Chiampi. Sixteen points in less than fifty final seconds let the Harvards tie the favored

Elis. Cosmic equipoise. And cause for celebration. Mellifluid melodies were wafting everywhere.

> *Resistless our team sweeps goalward*
> *With the fury of the blast.*
> *We'll fight for the name of Harvard*
> *Till the last white line is past.*

There was no further talk of family tradition on that occasion. Footballism filled the air. We lauded Chiampi, Gatto and the Crimson line. We toasted Harvard's first unbeaten season since before my father entered college (!).

Now, one November later, all was different. Solemn. Not because we'd lost the contest. But because, in fact, a whole entire year had passed. And still the question lingered open. Actually, by now it gaped.

"Father, I'm a lawyer, and I feel commitments. If you will, responsibilities."

"I understand. But Boston as a base of operations wouldn't totally preclude involvement with your social causes. Quite the opposite; you might conceive of working in the Firm as activism from the other side."

I didn't want to hurt him. So I didn't say that what he called "the other side" was to a great extent what I'd been fighting.

"I can see your point," I said, "but frankly . . ."

Now I hesitated, long enough to smooth my vehement objections into nonabrasive words.

"Father, I appreciate your asking. But I'm sort of, really, well . . . extremely . . . disinclined."

I guess I'd been definitive. Father didn't add his usual request to think about it.

"I understand," he said. "I'm disappointed, but I understand."

On the turnpike back, I felt sufficiently relieved to banter with myself:

"One tycoon per family's enough."

And hoped that Marcie was at home by now.

28

"Oliver, how sure are you?"

"Marcie, I am positive."

She was waiting when I got back from New Haven, looking like a freshly made soufflé. You'd never think she'd spent the whole day on a flight from coast to coast.

Though the conversation with my father was among a multitude of topics I reported, it aroused her interest.

"You said no, right out of hand?"

"And out of mind," I said, "and of conviction."

Then I remembered whom I was addressing.

"Naturally, if you were in my place, you'd take the damn thing over, wouldn't you? I mean I guess that's what you did."

"But I was angry," Marcie said sincerely. "I was out to prove a lot of things."

"So am I. And that's exactly why I turned it down."

"And you're willing to let . . . well . . . a heritage die out?"

"Some heritage—America's first sweatshops!"

"Oliver, that's ancient history. Nowadays a union worker earns fantastic—"

"That's beside the point."

"And look at all the good your family's done! The hospital, the hall at Harvard. Contributions—"

"Look, let's not discuss it, huh?"

"Why not? You're being juvenile! You're like some flaming radical in retrospect!"

Why the hell was she so passionately pushing me to join the damn Establishment?

"Goddammit, Marcie!"

Suddenly the bell! That is, the ringing telephone called the antagonists to neutral corners.

"Should I answer?" Marcie said.

"The hell with it—it's nearly midnight."

"It could be important."

"Not for me," I said.

"I live here too," she said.

"Then answer it," I barked, pissed off that what I'd hoped would be an amorous reunion was now rancorous.

Marcie answered.

"It's for you," she said. And handed me the phone.

"Yeah, what?" I growled.

"Hey, terrific! She's still there!" a voice enthused.

Philip Cavilleri. And I had to smile.

"Are you checking up on me?"

"You want an honest answer? Yes. So how's it goin'?"

"What's your meaning, Philip?"

He replied with, "Ding dong, ding dong."

"What the hell is that—your cuckoo clock?"

"It's weddin' bells! When do they ring, goddammit?"

"Phil, you'll be the first to know."

"Then tell me now, so I can go to sleep in peace."

"Philip," I replied with feigned exasperation, "did you call me just to broadcast marriage propaganda or was there a further message?"

"Yeah. Let's talk some turkey."

"Phil, I told you—"

"I mean real-life turkey. Stuffed. Thanksgivin' birdies."

"Oh." Next week, of course, would be the holiday.

"I want you and that cultured female voice to join my fam'ly gathering on the Day of Grace."

"Who's coming to your gathering?" I asked.

"The Pilgrim Fathers! What the hell's the difference?"

"Whom have you invited, Philip?" I insisted, fearing hordes of overzealous Cranstonites.

"So far, only me," he said.

"Oh," I retorted. And remembered Philip couldn't bear to join his relatives on holidays. ("All those damn bambinos crying," he'd complain. And I would humor his alleged excuse.)

"Good. Then you can join us here. . . ." I glanced at Marcie, who encouraged me, while also semaphoring, "Who the hell will cook?"

"Marcie wants to meet you," I insisted.

"Oh, I couldn't," Philip said.

"Come on."

"Okay. What time?"

"Like early afternoon," I said. "Just let me know which train to meet."

"Can I bring some stuff? Remember I purvey Rhode Island's finest punkin pie."

"That's great."

"And stuffin' too."

"That's great."

Marcie signaled madly from the sidelines, "All the way!"

"Uh . . . Phil, there's just one thing. Do you know how to cook a turkey?"

"Like a Turk!" he said. "An' I could get a good one from my buddy Angelo. You sure she wouldn't mind?"

"Who, Phil?"

"Your lovely fiancée. Some ladies get resentful when a fella barges in their kitchen."

"Marcie's very loose on that," I said.

She now was jumping up and down for joy.

"That's great. Then she must truly be a lovely girl. 'Marcie,' huh? Hey, Oliver—you think she'll like me?"

"Positive."

"Then meet me at the train at half past ten. Okay?"

"Okay."

I was about to put the phone down when I heard him call:
"Say, Oliver?"
"Yes, Phil?"
"Thanksgivin' is a proper time to plan a weddin'."
"Nighty-night, Phil."
We at last had signed off. I looked at Marcie.
"Are you glad he's coming?"
"If you think he'll like me."
"Hey—no sweat."
"I've got a better chance if I don't cook."
We smiled. There was a grain of truth in that.
"Wait a minute, Oliver," she said. "Aren't you expected up in Ipswich?"
True enough. Thanksgiving was a Barrett Holy Day. But *force majeure.*
"I'll call and say I'm caught up in that School Board case which starts on Monday."
And Marcie also had to make some changes.
"I should be in Chicago, but I'll fly here for the dinner and then take the last plane back. Thanksgiving is a crucial day on retail calendars. The sales start Friday."
"Good. It'll mean a lot to Phil."
"I'm glad," she said.
"Okay, now that everything is organized," I said facetiously, "may I express emotions?"
"Yes. What sort?"
"Well . . . sadness. Harvard lost to Yale. It's been a wretched day. Could you remotely think of some way you might comfort me?"
"You need therapy," she said. "Would you be willing to stretch out upon the bed?"
"I would," I said. And did. She sat down on the edge.
"Now do whatever comes to mind," she said.
I did.
And we slept happily ever after.

All that week Phil Cavilleri labored ceaselessly preparing festive dainties. And he spent a fortune on investigative calls.

"Does she like walnuts in her stuffin'?"

"She's at work now, Phil."

"At eight P.M.?"

"She works on Wednesday night," I said by way of quasi-explanation.

"What's the number there?" he asked, alacritous to learn her preference in nuts.

"She's busy, Phil. But yes—I just remembered. Walnuts really turn her on."

"That's great!"

And off he went. For then.

But in the days that followed we had conference calls concerning mushrooms, what type squash, the style of cranberries (the jelly or whole fruit?) and all the vegetables.

"They'll be strictly from the farm," I was assured long-distance from Rhode Island. "What you people in New York get is just frozen crap."

Naturally, I fabricated all of Marcie's big decisions. This was her week for Cincinnati, Cleveland and Chicago. Though we spoke at frequent intervals, and for at least an hour each evening, menus for Thanksgiving had a low priority.

"How's the School Board preparation, friend?"

"I'm ready. Barry's research is terrific. All I have to do is argue. Meanwhile I'm rereading all the banned material. They won't let junior high school kids read Vonnegut. Or even *Catcher in the Rye!*"

"Oh, that book was sad," said Marcie. "Poor sweet lonely Holden Caulfield."

"Don't you feel for me? I'm lonely too."

"Oh, Oliver, I don't just feel for you. I grope."

If by some chance my phone was being tapped, the tapper surely got his rocks off every night when Marcie called.

On Thanksgiving morn I was awakened by a turkey at the door. Waving it was Philip Cavilleri, who'd decided at the final moment that a *really* early train was needed. To allow sufficient time for him to set a proper feast. ("I know your lousy oven—it reminds me of a ruptured toaster.")

"Hey, where is she?" Philip asked, the moment he'd put down his load of goodies. (He was semi-peeking almost everywhere.)

"Phil, she doesn't live here. And besides, she's in Chicago."

"Why?"

"On business."

"Oh. She works in business?"

"Yes."

He was impressed. And then he quickly asked:

"Does she *appreciate* you, Oliver?"

Jesus, he would never stop!

"Come on, Phil, let's get to work."

I cleaned. He cooked. I set the table. He dished out whatever would be served up cold. By noon the banquet was in readiness. Except the turkey, timed to ripen juicily at half past four. Marcie's plane would reach La Guardia by half past three. Since there would be no traffic on the holiday, we'd easily sit down to eat by five. While we waited, Phil and I devoured TV football. He refused to take the briefest walk, although the weather was November crisp and sunny. The dedicated pro, he always had to be in basting distance of the Bird.

Slightly after two, there was the telephone.

"Oliver?"

"Where are you, Marcie?"

"At the airport. In Chicago. I can't come."

"Is something wrong?"

"Not here. But there's a crisis in the Denver store. I'm flying there in twenty minutes. I'll explain tonight."

"Is it serious?"

"Yeah, I guess. It may take several days, but if we're lucky we can save the ship."

"How can I help?" I asked.

"Well . . . please explain to Philip. Tell him that I'm really sorry."

"Okay. But that won't be easy."

Minipause. Which would have been much longer were she not in haste to catch her plane.

"Hey, you sound slightly pissed."

I weighed my words. I didn't want to aggravate her problems.

"Only disappointed, Marce. I mean we—never mind."

"Please hang in there till I get to Denver. It'll take some long explaining."

"Yeah," I said.

"Say something nice, please, Oliver."

"I hope they serve you turkey on your flight."

There was some consolation in my solo feast with Phil.

It was like old times. We were together, just the two of us.

The food was wonderful. It's just my thoughts were rather difficult to swallow.

Philip tried to help me brave it.

"Look," he said, "such things can happen in the world of business. Business people travel. It's the nature of . . . the business."

"Yeah."

"Besides, there's other people who can't make it home. Like soldiers . . ."

Great analogy!

"And if they made her stay away, that must mean Marcie is important, right?"

I didn't answer.

"Has she some executive position?"

"Sort of."

"Well, that's to her credit. She's a modrun girl. Christ, you should be proud. She's an achiever. Is she bucking for promotion?"

"In a way."

"That's good. Ambitious. That's to be proud of, Oliver."

I nodded. Just to show I wasn't sleeping.

"When I was growin' up," quoth Phil, "a family took pride to say, 'My kid's ambitious.' Of course they usta say it of the fellas. But these modrun girls, they're equal, ain't they?"

"Very," I replied.

At last my taciturnity convinced him that he couldn't mitigate my disappointment.

"Hey," he said, and shifted to another gear. "It wouldn't be this way if you would marry her."

"Why not?" I was as light on irony as possible.

"Because a woman is a woman. Wives gotta be at home here with their families. It's nature's way."

I would not dispute his philosophy of nature.

"Look," he said, "it's your own goddamn fault. If you would make an honest woman of her—"

"Phil!"

"What's true is true," he barked, defending someone he had never met. "Those woman's-lib Comanches can throw pies at me, but I know what the Bible says. A man an' woman gotta *cleave* together. Right?"

"Right," I said, and hoped that it would shut him up. It did. For several seconds.

"Hey, what the hell does 'cleave' mean, anyway?" he asked.

"Hold very close," I answered.

"Has she read the Bible, Oliver?"

"I guess so."

"Call her up. There's bound to be a Gideon in her hotel."

"I will," I said.

"What are your feelings?"

Dr. London, here's a time I really need your help. My feelings?

"Anger. Rage. Pissed off."

But also more.

"Confused. I don't know what to feel. We're on the verge of . . . I don't know."

Yeah, I *did* know, but couldn't say it.

"I mean . . . building a relationship. Or trying to. How can we tell if it can really work if we don't have the time together? Time in person. Not just on the telephone. I'm not the slightest bit religious, but if I thought that we'd be separated Christmas Eve, I'd . . ."

Maybe cry? I'm sure that even Jack the Ripper spent the Yule with friends.

"Look, the problem's serious. I mean the Denver store's got shaky management. Marcie *had* to go. She has to stay. It's nothing she can delegate. And who the hell's suggesting she should delegate? To hold my hand? To cook my breakfast?

"Dammit—it's her job! I've got to live with that. I'm not complaining. All right, sure I am. But I'm the one who's immature. . . .

"And maybe more than that. I'm selfish. Inconsiderate. Marcie is my . . . we're a . . . sort of couple. She's got hasslement in

Denver. Truly. Even though she is the boss, some wise-ass locals think she's got a heavy hand. It's not that easy.

"Meanwhile I'm just lounging here and moaning over nothing, when I maybe should be *there* to back her up. A little personal support. Christ, I know what it would mean to *me*. And if I did, she'd really know . . ."

I hesitated. How much was I telling Dr. London with my incompleted sentences?

"I think I ought to fly to Denver."

Silence. I was pleased with my decision. Then I realized this was Friday.

"On the other hand, next Monday I'm supposed to go to trial against that School Board. I've been dying to get in there with those Yahoos . . ."

Pause for introspection. Weigh your values, Oliver.

"Okay, I could give the ball to Barry Pollack. Actually, he's deeper into it than I. Of course, he's younger. They might rattle him. Ah, shit, I know *I'd* make it stronger. It's important!"

Christ, what a ferocious game of psychic Ping-Pong. I was dazed from hearing my own counterarguments!

"But dammit, Marcie's more important! Never mind how cool she is, she's out there all alone and she could use a friend. And maybe I could—once in my whole life—consider someone other than my goddamn self!"

I was convinced by my last argument. I think.

"I fly to Denver, right?"

I looked at the doctor. London pondered for a moment and replied:

"If not, I'll see you five o'clock on Monday."

30

"Oliver, don't leave me—I'll crack up."

"Don't worry, it'll be all right. Stay loose."

Bouncing over potholes in a taxi to the airport, I was tranquilizing Barry Pollack for his day in court.

"But, Ollie, *why?* Why pull this sudden fade-out on me *now?*"

"You'll handle it. You know the research upside down."

"I know I *know* my stuff. But, Oliver, I can't debate and bullshit anywhere like you. They'll foul me up. We'll lose!"

I soothed him and explained how he could parry all the opposition's thrusts. Remember, speak distinctly. Very slowly. Baritone, if possible. And always call our expert witness "doctor"; it impresses them.

"Christ, I'm scared. Why must you go to Denver *now?*"

"It's necessary, Bar. I can't be more specific."

We bounced in nervous silence for a mile.

"Hey, Ol?"

"Yeah, Bar?"

"Will you tell me, if I guess what's going on?"

"Yeah. Maybe."

"It's an offer. A fantastic offer. Right?"

Just then we reached the terminal. I was halfway out before the taxi stopped.

"Well, *is* it?" Barry asked. "Is it an offer?"

Oliver the Cheshire Cat shook hands with his young colleague through the taxi window.

"Hey—good luck to both of us."

I turned and headed for the check-in desk. God bless you, Barry—you were shaking so, you didn't notice I was edgy too. *Because I hadn't told her I was coming.*

No sooner did we land in Mile High City (as the jolly pilot endlessly referred to it), I grabbed my little suitcase, picked a cabby who looked like he'd drive extremely fast and said, "Brown Palace. Please shake ass."

"Then hold yer old sombrero, buddy," he replied. I'd chosen well.

By 9 P.M. (eleven minutes later) we were at the Palace, Denver's venerable hostelry. It has a massive lobby, sort of a *fin de siècle* astrodome. The floors are piled in tiers with one huge garden in the middle. You get dizzy merely looking at the hollowness above.

I knew her suite from all those phone calls. I deposited my luggage at the desk and started jogging toward the seventh floor. I didn't call the room.

I took a second just to catch my breath (the altitude). Then knocked.

There was silence.

Then a man appeared. If I may say, a very handsome man. A plastic prince.

"May I help you?"

Who the hell was he? His accent wasn't Denver. It was pseudo-English via Mars.

"I'd like to speak to Marcie," I replied.

"I'm afraid she's busy at the moment."

With what? What had I stumbled into? This guy was too beautiful. The kind of face you want to punch on principle.

"I'd like to see her anyway," I said.

He had about two inches on me height-wise. And his suit was so well made I couldn't tell where it left off and he began.

"Mm, are you expected by Miss Binnendale?" His way of saying "Mm" could be the prelude to a broken jaw.

Before I could continue with polemics or with punches, a female voice floated from within.

"What is it, Jeremy?"

"Nothing, Marcie. A mistake."

He turned to me again.

"Jeremy, I'm no mistake," I said. "My parents wanted me." Either the effect of wit, or else the menace in my tone, made Jeremy step back and let me enter.

I wondered as I strode the little corridor how Marcie would react. And what the hell she might be in the midst of.

The living room was wall-to-wall gray flannel.

Which is to say, executives were scattered everywhere, each by an ashtray, puffing nervously or chewing cardboard sandwiches.

At a desk, unsmoking and uneating (also not undressed, as I had feared), was Marcie Binnendale. I'd caught her in the flagrant midst of . . . business.

"Do you know this gentleman?" said Jeremy.

"Indeed," said Marcie, smiling. But not flying to my arms, as I had dreamed en route.

"Hello," I said. "I'm sorry if I interrupted."

Marcie looked around, and then said to her platoon, "Excuse me for a moment."

She and I went to the corridor. I took her hand, but Marcie gently kept me from a grasp of more.

"Hey—what are you doing here?"

"I thought you'd need a friend. I'll stay until you settle things."

"But what about your lawsuit?"

"Screw it. You were more important." And I grabbed her waist.

"Are you berserk?" she whispered, anything but angry.

"Yeah. Berserk from sleeping—or not sleeping—in a double bed alone. Berserk from missing you across the plywood toast and soggy eggs. Berserk—"

"Hey, friend," she said, and pointed to the other room, "I'm in a meeting."

Who gave a shit what all the flannelites could hear. I ranted on. "—and I was wondering if even in your presidential turmoil, you might also feel a little bit berserk and—"

"Schmuck," she whispered sternly, "I am in a meeting."

"I can see you're busy, Marce. But look—just take your time, and when you're finished, I'll be waiting in my room."

"This could last forever. . . ."

"Then I'll wait forever."

Marcie dug the sound of that.

"Okay, my friend."

She kissed me on the cheek. And then went back to her affairs.

"Oh, my love, my Aphrodite, my exquisite rhapsody . . ."

Jean-Pierre Aumont, a Foreign Legion officer, was putting it to some pneumatic desert princess, who was gasping, "Non non non, beware mon père!"

It was after midnight and this ancient movie was the only game in town on Denver television.

Otherwise, my company was a diminishing supply of Coors. I was so punchy I was talking to the screen.

"For Christ's sake, Jean-Pierre, just rip off her costume!" He paid no heed to me and kept the bullshit—and his hands—too high.

Until a knock.

Thank God.

"Hi, baby," Marcie said.

She was tired-looking, and her hair was semi-loose. The way I like it.

"How's it going?"

"I sent everybody home."

"Did you solve it all?"

"Oh, no. It's still a hopeless mess. May I come in?"

I was so exhausted I was slouching in the doorway, sort of blocking her.

She came in. Took off her shoes. Flopped on the bed. And then looked wearily at me.

"You big romantic schmuck. You punted that important case?"

I smiled.

"I had priorities," I answered. "You were off in Denver in a bind. And I just thought you needed someone to be there with you."

"It's nice," she said. "It's slightly crazy, but it's awful nice."

I got into the bed and took her in my arms.

In roughly fifteen seconds we were both asleep.

I had this dream: that Marcie slipped into my tent and while I slumbered, whispered, "Oliver, we're gonna spend the day together. Just the two of us. And get as high as possible."

When I awoke I saw a dream come true.

Marcie stood there, dressed for snow. And in her hand a ski suit that might just fit me.

"Come on," she said. "We're going to a mountain."

"But what about your meeting?"

"It's with *you* today. I'll reconvene the others after dinner."

"Jesus, Marcie, what's got into you?"

"Priorities." She smiled.

Marcie knocked a person's head off.

The victim was a snowman and the cause of death decapitation by a snowball.

"What's the next game?" I inquired.

"I'll tell you after lunch," she said.

Where precisely in the vast expanse of Rocky Mountain Park we now were camping, I had no idea. But nothing animate was visible from us to the horizon. And the loudest noise was footsteps crunching snow. Unadulterated whiteness everywhere. Like nature's wedding cake.

She maybe couldn't light a city stove, but Marcie was fantastic with a can of Sterno. We dined on soup and sandwich in the Rockies. Screw all fancy restaurants. And all legal obligations. And all telephones. And any city population more than two.

"Where exactly are we?" (Marcie had the compass.)

"Sort of slightly east of Nowhere in Particular."

"I like the neighborhood."

"And if you hadn't pulled your bull-in-china-shop routine, I'd still be back in Denver in a smoke-filled room."

She made coffee on the Sterno. Experts might have called it not too good or barely drinkable, and yet it made me warm.

"Marcie," I said, only half in jest, "you are a closet cook."

"But only in the wilderness . . ."

"Then that's your place in life."

She looked at me. Then looked around and radiated happiness.

"I wish we didn't have to leave," she said.

"We don't," I answered.

And my tone was serious.

"Marcie, we could stay here till the glaciers melted, or until we wanted to comb beaches. Or canoe the Amazon. I mean it."

She hesitated. Pondering how to react to my—what was it? A suggestion? A proposal?

"Are you sort of testing me or are you sort of serious?" she asked.

"I'm sort of both. I could be seduced to quit the rat race, couldn't you? I mean not many people have our options. . . ."

"Come on, Barrett," she protested, "you're the most ambitious guy I've ever met. Except for me. I bet you even dream of being President."

I smiled. But presidential timber cannot tell a lie.

"Okay. I did. But lately I've been thinking I would rather teach my kids to ice-skate."

"Really?"

Not facetious, she was honestly surprised.

"Only if they want to learn," I added. "Couldn't you get pleasure out of something noncompetitive?"

She thought a second.

"It certainly would be a new experience," she answered. "Till you came along I only got my rocks off from those look-at-me type victories. . . ."

"Tell me what you think would make you happy *now*."

"A guy," she said.

"What kind?"

"Who wouldn't wholly buy my act, I guess. Who'd understand that what I really want is . . . not to always be the boss."

I waited, while the mountains sat in silence, offering no comment.

"You," she said at last.

"I'm glad," I answered.

"What should we do now, Oliver?"

We were high on quiet. And our sentences were punctuated with reflective pauses.

"Wanna know what you should do?" I said.

"Yes."

I breathed deeply and then told her.

"Sell the stores."

She nearly dropped her coffee.

"Whaat?"

"Listen, Marcie, I could write a thesis on the life style of a store-chain president. It's constant motion, constant changes, fire engine always ready in the driveway."

"All too true."

"Well, that may be great for business, but relationships are just the opposite. They need lots of time and very little motion."

Marcie didn't answer. So I lectured on.

"Therefore," I said blithely, "sell all your stores. We'll get a lush consultancy for you in any city you would like. I can chase the ambulances anywhere. Then maybe we could both grow roots. And grow some other little things."

"You're dreaming." Marcie laughed.

"And you are full of shit," I answered. "You're still too much in love with your own power."

This was not expressed in tones accusatory. Though it was the goddamn truth.

"Hey," she said, "you tested me."
"I did," I answered, "and you flunked."
"You're arrogant and selfish," she said playfully.
I nodded yes. "I'm also human."
Marcie looked at me. "But will you stick with me . . . ?"
"The snow has gotta melt," I said.
And then we rose, hiked arm in arm back to the car.
And drove to Denver. Where there wasn't any snow at all.

It was Wednesday evening by the time we reached New York.
Marcie'd set her Denver house in order by that morning and we
even toyed with going for another snowball fight. But superego
triumphed. It was time to work again. And I could even give
some help to Barry Pollack in the homestretch (we had kept in
touch by phone).

The line for cabs was endless and we froze our heels. At last
our turn arrived. And right before us stood a crumpled piece of
yellow tin. In other words, a New York taxi.

"I won't go to Queens," the driver growled in greeting.

"I won't either," I replied, while yanking at his mutilated door,
"so let's try twenty-three East Sixty-fourth."

We both were in now. He was legally enjoined to take us to
our stated destination.

"Let's try five-oh-four East Eighty-sixth."

What?

This was Marcie's startling suggestion.

"Who the hell lives there?" I asked.

"We do." She smiled.

"We *do?*"

"What are you, buddy," said the cabby, "an amnesiac?"

"What are you, cabby," I retorted, "Woody Allen?"

"At least I can remember where I live," he said in self-defense.

By now the cabby's fellow cabbies were encouraging his swift departure with a loud cacophony of horns and curses.

"Okay—*where?*" he now demanded.

"East Eighty-sixth," said Marcie. And then whispered to me she'd explain en route. To say the least, it took me by surprise.

In military terms it's called a DMZ—the area where neither army can deploy its forces. This was Marcie's notion in selecting an apartment that would be not hers, not mine, not even ours, but rather neutral territory.

Okay. That made sense. My rat house was a bit too much. And she had stood the test of grime.

"Well?" said Marcie.

Unequivocally, the place was great. I mean it looked exactly like those perfect layouts on the upper floors of Binnendale's. I'd watched young couples gazing at those model rooms, and dreaming, "Gee, if we could live like this."

Marcie took me through the living room, the gadget-laden kitchen ("I'll take cooking lessons, Oliver"), her future office, then the king-size bedroom and, at last, the big surprise: *my* office.

Yes. We had separate rooms for His and Her professions. Mine was furnished in a herd of leather. Shelves of glass and chrome to hold my legal books. Sophisticated lighting. Everything.

"Well?" said Marcie, clearly wanting me to burst into a song.

"It's unreal," I said.

And wondered why I felt like we were on a stage set reading from a script. By her.

And why that should make any difference.

"What are your feelings?"

Dr. London hadn't changed his methods in my absence.

"Look, we share the rent."

Come on, I told myself, who pays is not a feeling. And it wasn't even what was really on my mind.

"It isn't ego, Doctor. But the way she likes to . . . manage both our lives."

A pause.

"Look, I don't need a decorator. Or romantic lighting. Can't she understand all that is bullshit? Jenny bought us beat-up furniture, a creaking bed and a crummy table, *all* for ninety-seven bucks! The only dinner guests we ever had were roaches. It was windy in the winter. We could smell what all our neighbors had for dinner. It was utter grunge!"

Another pause.

"But we were *happy* and I never really noticed. Yeah, I noticed when the bed leg broke—'cause we were in it. And we laughed."

Another pause. Oliver, what is it that you're saying?

I think I'm saying that I don't like Marcie's new apartment.

Yes, my brand-new office *is* a showplace. But when I have to think, I go back to my old basement. Where the books still are. And where the bills still come. And where, when Marcie's out of town, I still bunk out.

And inasmuch as we are in a Christmas countdown situation, Marcie is conspicuously absent. In Chicago at the moment.

And I'm feeling bad.

Because I have to work tonight. And I can't do so in the dream house there on Eighty-sixth Street. Because New York is decked with boughs of holly. And I'm feeling lousy even though I now have *two* apartments to be lonely in. And I'm ashamed to call Phil just to talk. For fear of having to admit that I'm alone.

So here it is December 12, Barrett working in his subterranean retreat in search of precedents in musty volumes. And longing for a time he can't retrieve.

When work could palliate, benumb, indeed preoccupy. But thanks to new-acquired powers of psychic *intro*spection, I can't *extro*spect. I mean I just can't concentrate. I'm wallowing in *me* instead of *Meister* v. *Georgia*.

And because the Muzak in my office elevator daily cannonades my ears with carols, I have a Yuletide schizophrenia.

Here's the problem, Doctor. (I am talking to myself, but since I value my opinion, I refer to me as Doctor.)

God—in his capacity as Judge of the Celestial Court—has reaffirmed the following as law:

Thou shalt be home for Christmas.

I may be easy on some other of the good Lord's legislation, but I bend to this one.

Barrett, thou art homesick, ergo thou hadst better—dammit—make some plans.

But, Doctor, there's the problem.

Where is home?

("Where the heart is, naturally. That will be fifty dollars, please.")

Thank you, Doctor. For another fifty, may I ask:

Where is my goddamn heart?

It isn't that I didn't sometimes know.

I was a little kid once. I liked getting gifts and trimming trees.

I was a husband and though Jenny was agnostic ("Oliver, I wouldn't hurt His feelings and say 'atheist' "), she'd come home from her two jobs and we would have a party with each other. Singing bawdy variations on the Yuletide lyrics.

Which still says a lot for Christmas. 'Cause together is together and that's what the evening always made us.

Meanwhile it is half past nine, some dozen shopping days to Christmas and I'm out of it already. For, as I said, I have this problem.

Christmas can't be spent in Cranston as of late. My friend there says he's joined an over-forties cruise instead. ("Who knows what it could lead to?") It is Phil's impression that he's made things easier. But he sails off and leaves me on the dock of a dilemma.

Ipswich, Massachusetts, where my parents live, lays claim to being home for me.

Marcie Binnendale, with whom I live when she's in striking distance, argues that the stockings should be hung on Eighty-sixth Street.

I would like to be where I won't feel alone. But somehow sense that both these options offer merely half a loaf.

Ah—wait! There is a legal precedent for halving loaves! The judge, I think, was Solomon (his first name, King). His watershed decision would be my solution.

Christmas spent with Marcie.

But in Ipswich, Massachusetts.

Falalalala lalalala.

"Hello, Mother."

"How are you, Oliver?"

"I'm fine. How's Father?"

"Fine."

"That's fine. Uh—it's about—uh—Christmas."

"Oh, I do hope *this* time—"

"Yes," I instantly assured her, "we'll be there. I mean—uh—Mother, may I bring a guest? Uh—if there's room."

Idiotic question!

"Yes, of course, dear."

"It's a friend."

That's brilliant, Oliver. She might have thought it was an enemy.

"Oh," Mother said, unable to conceal emotion (not to mention curiosity). "That's fine."

"From out of town. We'd have to put her up."

"That's fine," said Mother. "Is it someone . . . that we know?" In other words, who is her family?

"No one that we have to make a fuss for, Mother."

That would fake her out!

"That's fine," she said.

"I'll drive up early Christmas Eve. Marcie will be flying from the Coast."

"Oh."

Considering my history, my mother doubtless thought it might be from the Coast of Timbuktu.

"Well, we'll look forward to you and Miss . . ."

"Nash. Marcie Nash."

"We'll look forward to your visit."

It is mutual. And that, as Dr. London will attest, is quite a feeling.

~~~~~~

Why?

I could imagine Marcie's ruminations as she jetted from Los Angeles to Boston on December 24. The quintessence would be *why*.

Why has he invited me to meet his parents? And for Christmas. Does this gesture mean he's getting . . . serious?

Naturally, we'd never broached such matters with each other. But I'm fairly confident that up there in the stratosphere a certain Bryn Mawr intellectual is pondering hypotheses to figure out her New York roommate's motivations.

And yet she never brought it to the surface and inquired, "Oliver—why did you ask me?"

I'm glad. For frankly, I'd have answered, "I don't know."

It had been a hasty impulse, typical of me. Calling home before consulting Marcie. Or my own inner thoughts. (Though Marcie really twinkled when I asked her.)

I was also hasty in the self-deceiving message I transmitted to my brain: It's just a friend you happen to be going with and Christmas happens to be now. There's no significance and no "intention" whatsoever.

Bullshit.

Oliver, you know damn well it isn't too ambiguous when you invite a girl to meet your parents. Over Christmas.

Buddy, it is not the sophomore prom.

All this seemed so lucid now. One full week later. As I paced the Logan Airport terminal in sympathetic circles with her pilot's holding pattern.

In real life, Oliver, what would such a gesture intimate?

Now, after several days of probing, I could answer consciously. It hints of marriage. Matrimony. Wedlock. Barrett, dost thou take this whirlwind . . . ?

Which would therefore make the trip to Ipswich something that would fill some atavistic craving for parental approbation. *Why* do I still care what Mom and Daddy think?

Do you love her, Oliver?

Jesus, what a stupid time to ask yourself!

Yeah? Another inner voice shouts, This *is* the very time to ask!

Do I love her?

It's too complicated for a simple yes or no.

Then why the hell am I so sure I want to *marry* her?

Because . . .

Well, maybe it's irrational. But somehow I believe a real commitment would provide the catalyst. The ceremony would evoke the "love."

"Oliver!"

The first one off the plane turned out to be the subject of my thoughts. Who looked fantastic.

"Hey, I really missed you, friend," she said, her hand caressing underneath my jacket. Though I held her just as tight, I couldn't wander anatomically. We were in *Boston*, after all. But wait till later. . . .

"Where's your little bag?" I asked.

"I've got a bigger one. It's checked."

"Oho. Will we be treated to a fashion show?"

"Nothing too far out," she answered. Thus acknowledging her wardrobe had been planned with mucho thought.

She was carrying an oblong package.

"I'll take that," I offered.

"No, it's fragile," she replied.

"Ah, your heart," I quipped.

"Not quite," she answered. "Just your father's present."

"Oh."

"I'm nervous, Oliver," she said.

We had traversed the Mystic River Bridge and were enmeshed in Route 1 Christmas traffic.

"You're full of crap," I said.

"What if they don't like me?" she continued.

"Then we'll just exchange you after Christmas," I replied.

Marcie pouted. Even so, her face was gorgeous.

"Say *something* reassuring, Oliver," she asked.

"I'm nervous too," I said.

Down Groton Street. The Gate. Then into our domain. And down the lengthy entrance road. The trees were barren, though the atmosphere kept something of a sylvan hush.

"It's peaceful," Marcie said. (She could have called it grossly vast, as I had dubbed her place, but she was far above such pettiness.)

"Mother, this is Marcie Nash."

If nothing else, her former husband had the perfect name. Exquisite in its blandness and evocative of zilch.

"We're happy, Marcie, you could be with us," my mother said. "We've looked forward to meeting you."

"I'm grateful that you asked me down."

What resplendent bullshit! Eye-to-eye with artificial smiles, these well-bred ladies mouthed the platitudes that buttress our whole social structure. Then went on to how-you-must-be-tired-after-such-a-journey, and how-*you*-must-be-exhausted-after-all-your-Christmas-preparations.

Father entered and they ran the selfsame gamut. Except he couldn't help betraying that he found her beautiful. Then, since —by the rule book—Marcie *must* be tired, she ascended to the guest room for some freshening.

We sat there. Mother, Father, I. We asked each other how we'd been and learned we'd all been fine. Which, naturally, was fine to hear. Would Marcie ("Charming girl," said Mother) be too weary to go caroling? It's awfully cold out.

"Marcie's tough," I answered, maybe meaning more than just her constitution. "She could carol in a blizzard."

"Preferably," Marcie said, reentering in what the skiers will be wearing up at St. Moritz this year, "all that wind would cover up my off-key singing."

"It doesn't matter, Marcie," said my mother, taking things a bit too literally. "It's the *esprit* that counts."

Mother never lost an opportunity to substitute an English word with French. She'd had two years at Smith, goddammit, and it showed.

"That outfit's splendid, Marcie," Father said. And I'm convinced he marveled at the way the tailoring did not disguise her . . . structure.

"It keeps out the wind," said Marcie.

"It can be *very* cold this time of year," my mother added.

Notice that one can go through a long and happy life discussing nothing but the weather.

"Oliver forewarned me," Marcie said.

Her tolerance for small talk was amazing. Like volleying with marshmallows.

At seven-thirty we joined two dozen of the Ipswich high-class riffraff by the church. Our oldest caroler was Lyman Nichols, Harvard, '10 (age seventy-nine), the youngest Amy Harris, merely five. She was the daughter of my college classmate, Stuart.

Stuart was the only guy I'd ever seen undazzled by my date. How could he think of Marcie? He was clearly so in love with little Amy (much reciprocated) and with Sara, who had stayed at home with ten-month Benjamin.

I suddenly was palpably aware of motion in my life. I *felt* time passing. And my heart was sad.

Stuart had a station wagon, so we drove with him. I held Amy on my lap.

"You're very lucky, Oliver," said Stu.

"I know," I answered.

Marcie, as required, indicated jealousy.

Hark, the herald angels sing . . .

Our repertoire was just as well worn as our route: the Upper Crusty members of the congregation, who would greet our musical appearance with polite applause, some feeble punch, and milk and cookies for the kids.

Marcie dug the whole routine.

"This is *country*, Oliver," she said.

By half past nine, we'd all but finished our appointed rounds (a Christmas pun, ho ho), and as tradition bade, concluded at the ducal manor, Dover House.

Oh come, all ye faithful . . .

I watched my father and my mother looking out at us. And wondered as I saw them smile. Is it because I'm standing next to Marcie? Or had little Amy Harris caught their hearts as she had mine?

Food and drink was better at our place. In addition to the cow juice, there was toddy for the frozen adults. ("You're the savior," Nichols, '10, said, patting Father on the back.)

Everybody left soon after.

I filled my tank with toddy.

Marcie drank some expurgated eggnog.

"I loved that, Oliver," she said, and took my hand.

I think my mother noticed. And was not upset. My father was, if anything, a trifle envious.

We trimmed the tree and Marcie complimented Mother on the beauty of the ornaments. She recognized the crystal of the star.

("It's lovely, Mrs. Barrett. It looks Czech."

"It is. My mother bought it just before the war.")

Then came other of the ancient venerated trinkets (some from ages I'd prefer our family forgot). As they draped the strands of popcorn and cranberries on the branches, Marcie coyly noted, "Someone must have *slaved* to make those garlands."

At which Father caught the ball with ease.

"My wife's done little else all week."

"Oh, really." Mother blushed.

I just sat there, not that hot for trimming, sipping warm and soothing liquid, thinking: Marcie is romancing them.

Half past eleven, tree all garnished, gifts beneath, and my perennial wool stocking hung next to a new-old one for my guest. The time had come to say good night. At Mother's cue, we all ascended. On the landing we bade one another happy dreams of sugarplums.

"Good night, Marcie," Mother said.

"Good night and thank you," echoed back.

"Good night, dear," Mother said again. And kissed me on the cheek. A peck which I construed to mean that Marcie passed.

O.B. III and wife departed. Marcie turned.

"I'll sneak into your room," I said.

"Are you absolutely crazy?"

"No, I'm absolutely horny," I replied. "Hey, Marce, it's Christmas Eve."

"Your parents would be horrified," she said. And maybe meant it.

"Marcie, I'll bet even *they* make love tonight."

"They're married," Marcie said. And with a hasty kiss upon my lips, she disengaged and disappeared.

What the hell!

I shuffled to my ancient room, its adolescent décor (pennants and team pictures) all museumly intact. I wanted to call someone ship-to-shore and tell him, "Phil, I hope at least the action's good with you."

I didn't.

I went to bed confused about what I was hoping to receive for Christmas.

Good morning! Merry Christmas! Here's a package just for *you!*

Mother gave my father yet another batch of ties and Sea Island cotton handkerchiefs. They looked very much like every year's. But then so did the dressing gown my father gave my mother.

I got half a dozen of whatever ties the Brooks man said were right for youth.

Marcie got the latest Daphne Du Maurier from Mother.

I had spent my annual five minutes at Christmas shopping and my gifts reflected it. My mother got some handkerchiefs, my father yet more ties, and Marcie got a book: *The Joy of Cooking* (we'll see how she reacts).

The tension (relatively speaking) centered on what our guest had brought.

To start with, Marcie's offerings had not, like ours, been wrapped at home. They had been swathed professionally (at you-know-where) in California.

Mother got a light-blue cashmere scarf ("You shouldn't have").

Father got that oblong box, which turned out to be Château Haut-Brion '59.

"What splendid wine," he said. In truth he was no connoisseur. Our "cellar" had some Scotch for Father's guests, some sherry for my mother's, and a case or two of fairly good champagne for grand occasions.

I received a pair of gloves. Though they were elegant, I still resented wearing Marcie's present at arm's length. It was too damn impersonal.

("Would you have preferred a mink-lined jock?" she later asked.

"Yes—that's where I was coldest!")

To top it off, or rather bottom it, I got what I had always got from Father. I received a check.

Joy to the World . . .

To this processional, zestfully performed by Mr. Weeks, the organist, we entered church and headed for our pew. The house was full of all our "peers," who were in fact discreetly peering at our female guest. ("She isn't one of us," I'm sure they said.) No one turned to gaze overtly save for Mrs. Rhodes, whose ninety-odd—extremely odd—long years could license such behavior.

But the congregation did watch Mrs. Rhodes. And couldn't help but notice that she smiled after a thorough look at Marcie. Ah, the hag approves.

We sang politely (not as loudly as last evening) and we heard the Reverend Mr. Lindley drone the service. Father read the lesson and, give credit, did it well. He took his breaths at commas, not, like Lindley, everywhere.

The sermon, Lord have mercy, showed the reverend was in sync with world affairs. He made mention of the conflict out in Southeast Asia, bade us think—at Christmastide—how much the Prince of Peace was needed in a World at War.

Thank Heaven Lindley is asthmatic so his sermons are gasped mercifully brief.

All benedicted, we retired to the steps of church. To have a replay of the after Harvard–Yale game meetings. Save this morning everyone is sober.

"Jackson!" "Mason!" "Harris!" "Barrett!" "Cabot!" "Lowell!" God!

Things of minor consequence were mumbled in between articulations of the cronies' names. Mother also had some friends to greet. But in a quiet manner, natch.

Then all at once a voice distinctly bellowed:

"Maah-cie dear!"

I whirled and saw my date embracing someone.

It was someone antiquated or—despite the church—he would have swallowed teeth.

Instantly my parents were at hand to see who had saluted Marcie with such fervor.

Good old Standish Farnham still had Marcie in his arms.

"Oh, Uncle Standish, what a nice surprise!"

Mother seemed enthused. Was Marcie niece to this distinguished "one of us"?

"Maah-cie, what would bring a city gal like you out to these bahrbr'ous pahts?" asked Standish, *a*'s as broad as Boston Harbor.

"She's staying with us," Mother interposed.

"Oh, Alison, how fine," said Standish, and then winked at me. "Do gahd her from that rakish lad of yours."

"We keep her under glass," I answered wryly. And old Standish larfed.

"Are you two related?" I inquired, wishing Standish would remove his hand from Marcie's waist.

"Only by affection. Mr. Farnham and my father were in partnership," she said.

"Not pahtners," he insisted, "brothers."

"Oh," said Mother, clearly hoping for a juicy new detail.

"We had some hosses," Standish said. "I sold 'em when her father died. The fun went out."

"Indeed," my mother said, beneath her Christmas bonnet a Vesuvius of curiosity. (For Standish just *assumed* we knew who Marcie's daddy was.)

"If you have time, come over in the afternoon," old Farnham said in parting.

"I have to be in New York City, Uncle Standish."

"Ah—the busy little gal," he crowed. "Well, shame on you for sneaking into Boston like a criminal." He blew a kiss to her and turned to us.

"Be sure she eats. If I recall my little Maah-cie, she was always on a diet. Merry Christmas."

Then as an afterthought he called, "Keep up the good work, Maah-cie. We're all proud of you!"

Father drove us back in Mother's station wagon. And in pregnant silence.

Pre-Christmas dinner, Father cracked a bottle of champagne.

"To Marcie," said my mother.

We all raised our glasses. Marcie merely wet her lips. Quite out of character, I then proposed a toast to Jesus.

There were six of us. The four who rose this morning supplemented now by Geoff, my mother's nephew from Virginia, and Aunt Helen, spinster sister of my father's father, who, I think, recalls Methuselah when both of them were studying at Harvard. Helen's deaf and Geoffrey eats as if he had a tapeworm. So the conversation wasn't noticeably changed.

We praised the mighty bird.

"Tell Florence, don't tell me," my mother humbly said. "She was up at dawn to start it off."

"The stuffing's simply marvelous," my New York roommate effervesced.

"Ipswich oysters, after all," said Mother, pleased as punch.

We feasted, everything aplenty. I and Geoff competed to be glutton of the day.

And strangely now, a second bottle of champagne was opened. Though I vaguely was aware that only I and Father were imbibing. Actually, I was so vague because I had imbibed the most.

Florence's perennial mince pie, then coffee in the parlor made it 3 P.M.

I'd have to wait a bit before we started to New York. To let my stomach settle and my brain grow clear.

"Marcie, would you like to take a walk?" my mother asked.

"I'd love to, Mrs. Barrett."

And they did.

Meanwhile Auntie Helen snoozed, and Geoff went up to plug into the football on the tube.

That left my father and myself.

"I'd really like some cool air too," I said.

"I wouldn't mind a walk," my father answered.

As we put our coats on, and went out into the winter frost, I was aware that *I* had asked him for this promenade. I could have copped out with the football game like Geoff. But no, I wanted conversation. With my father.

"She's a lovely girl," he said. Unasked.

But yet I think that's what I hoped we would discuss.

"Thank you, Father," I replied. "I think so too."

"She seems . . . fond of you."

We were in the woods now. Framed by leafless trees.

"I'm . . . sort of fond of her," I said at last.

My father weighed each word. He wasn't used to my *receptiveness*. Conditioned by the years of my hostility, he doubtless thought I'd turn him off at any point. But gradually he came to realize that I wouldn't. Thus he dared to ask me, "Is it serious?"

We walked along. At last I looked at him and answered quietly.

"I wish I knew."

Although I had been vague and almost enigmatic, Father sensed that I had honestly expressed what I was feeling. That is, confusion.

"Is there . . . a problem?" he inquired.

I looked at him and nodded silently.

"I think I understand," he said.

How? I hadn't told him anything.

"Oliver, it's not unnatural that you would still be grieving."

Father's insight took me by surprise. Or had he merely guessed that his remark might . . . touch me?

"No, it isn't Jenny," I replied. "I mean I think I'm ready for . . ." Why was I telling this to *him?*

He didn't press. He waited for my thoughts to be complete.

After several moments he said softly, "You did say there was a problem?"

"It's her family," I answered.

"Oh," he said. "Is there . . . resistance?"

"On *my* part," I replied. "Her father . . ."

"Yes?"

". . . was Walter Binnendale."

"I see," he said.

And with those simple words concluded the most intimate communication of our lives.

"Did they like me?"

"I would say you snowed them."

We had reached the Massachusetts Turnpike. It was dark. Not a creature was stirring.

"Are you pleased?" she asked.

I didn't answer. Marcie had expected verbal cartwheels. And instead I focused on the empty road.

"What's the matter, Oliver?" she said at last.

"You were courting them."

She seemed surprised that this had irked me.

"What's wrong with that?"

I let a little temper show. "But why, goddammit? Why?"

A pause.

"Because I want to marry you," she said.

Fortunately she was driving. I was stunned by the directness of her words. But then she never minces them.

"Then try romancing *me!*" I said.

She let us drive along with just the wind for background music. Then she answered, "Is it still a courtship with the two of us? I should think we passed that stage a while ago."

"Hmm," I murmured in most noncommittal tones. Because I feared that total silence might imply assent.

"Well, where exactly *are* we, Oliver?" she asked.

"About three hours from New York," I said.

"What have I done, precisely?"

We had stopped for coffee at the HoJo's after Sturbridge.

I wanted to say: Not enough.

And yet I was sufficiently composed to keep inflammatory words in check.

Because I knew I had been shaken by her matrimonial announcement. And was in no shape to frame a rational response.

"Well, what have I done to piss you off?" she asked again.

I longed to say: It's what you haven't done.

"Forget it, Marcie. We're both tired."

"Oliver, you're angry at me. Why don't you communicate instead of brood!"

This time she was right.

"Okay," I started, drawing circles with my finger on the laminated table. "We've just spent two weeks apart. Even though we both were busy, I dreamed all that time of getting back with you—"

"Oliver—"

"I don't mean just in bed. I mean I craved your company. The two of us together . . ."

"Oh, come on," she said. "It was a Christmas madness up in Ipswich."

"It's not just this weekend. I mean all the time."

She looked at me. I had not raised my voice, but still betrayed my fury.

"Ah, we're back to all my voyages these past few weeks."

"We're not. I mean the next ten thousand weeks."

"Oliver," she said, "I thought what made us work was that we each respected that we had career commitments too."

She's right. But just in theory.

"Hey—try reaching for 'career commitments' when you're all alone at three A.M."

I sensed a women's lib-stick blow was imminent. But I was wrong.

"Hey," she softly answered, "I have. Lots of times."

She touched my hand.

"Yeah? And what's it like to feel just hotel pillows?" I inquired.

"Lousy," she replied.

We were always near the end zone, but we never scored. Wasn't it her turn to say let's change the game?

"How do you deal with lonely nights?" I asked.

"I tell myself I have no choice."

"Do you *believe* yourself?"

I sensed hostilities at hand, a kind of Armageddon of the life styles.

"What do you want from a woman, Oliver?"

The tone was gentle. And the question loaded.

"Love," I said.

"In other words, a clinging vine?"

"I'd settle for a few more evenings in the same apartment."

I would not be philosophical. Or let her in the slightest way invoke the nature of my marriage. Jenny also worked, goddammit.

"I thought the two of us were happy as a couple."

"Yeah, when we're *with* each other. But, Marce, it's not a goddamn inventory you replenish just by phone."

The irony of my commercial metaphors was unappreciated.

"You are saying one of us should tag along and be the other's nanny?"

"I would—if you *needed* me."

"Good Christ! I just came out and said I want to marry you!"

She looked tired and exasperated. And the moment really wasn't opportune.

"Let's go," I said.

I paid. We stepped outside and started toward the car.

"Oliver," said Marcie.

"Yeah?"

"Isn't it just possible that you're upset in retrospect? I mean because they *did* like me. And *didn't* jump for joy when you brought Jenny home?"

"No," I said. And buried her remark a million fathoms deep.

Marcie, to her credit, is a fighter.

All throughout our Christmas–New Year's truce, I sensed her inwardly preparing for a New Campaign. The foe, of course, was her own instinct to mistrust the world.

And mine.

Anyway, as much as possible she stayed at home and tried to run the show by telephone. No easy trick with that post-Christmas lunacy. But still she did. She fought long-distance. And we spent the nights together. And—amazingly—some afternoons.

Then she sprung the big one on me New Year's Eve. We were readying for the Simpsons' party (yeah, I'd stashed some Alka-Seltzer, just in case). As I was shaving, Marcie joined me in the mirror and enhanced the picture. She did not mince words.

"Are you prepared for a commitment, Oliver?"

"Like what?" I asked, a trifle wary.

"Like how about a little trip? In February."

"And I suppose you've chosen where." Don't be sarcastic, Oliver, she's worked at this.

"Stay loose—and keep an open mind," she said. "It's true I have to check the Hong Kong Fashion Show and—"

"Hong Kong!"

She had caught me with the carrot of the Orient! My smile was hemispheric.

"So you dig, my friend?"

"You said you had to work," I answered with suspicion.

"To merely show one's face is not exactly work. Besides, the week before is Chinese New Year. We could have a solo celebration. Then going home, we'd stop off in Hawaii."

"Well . . ." I said. But my expression broadcast: Holy shit! Then, ever cautious, I inquired:

"Do you have any business in Hawaii?"

"None. Unless you count collecting coconuts."

What a New Year's proposition!

"Well?" she said.

"I like it, Marce. Especially Hawaii. Quiet beaches . . . moonlight walks . . ."

"A sort of honeymoon," she said.

Intriguing phraseology. I wondered how intentional.

I didn't turn to her. Instead I checked the mirror for a glimpse of her expression.

It was fogged with steam.

I didn't get permission from the boss.

I got encouragement.

Not that they were happy to be rid of me. But I had never had a day's vacation since I joined the firm.

There would be some sacrifices, though. I couldn't get involved in certain cases. Like the two in Washington involving draft resisters, which were using work I'd done for *Webber* v. *Selective Service*. And in February when the Congress would decide on how to deal with the de facto segregation problem. So I had some a priori retrospective qualms.

"You're worried that the world will be set right while you're away"—Mr. Jonas smiled—"but I promise we'll reserve a few injustices for you."

"Thank you, sir."

"Be a little selfish, Oliver. You've earned it."

Even while preparing for the trip (the Hong Kong Tourist Office inundates you with material), I handled several cases for the Midnight Raiders. And I blew the whistle on a fraudulent consumer con. Barry Pollack (champion in the School Board case) was following it up.

"Hey, Marce, what was the Treaty of Nanking?"

"It sounds like *The Mikado*," she replied.

I would educate her over breakfast, over dinner, over toothpaste, even interrupt her at the office.

"The Treaty of Nanking, if you must know—"

"Oh, must I?"

"Yes. When the English outaggressed them in the Opium War—"

"Ah—opium." Her eyes lit up.

I ignored her levity and lectured on.

"—China had to give up Hong Kong to the British."

"Oh," she said.

"That's only the beginning," I replied.

"I see," said Marcie, "and the end will be that fighting lawyer Barrett's gonna make them give it back. That right?"

Her smile increased the candlepower in the room.

"What about your homework for the trip?" I asked.

"I've been there several times," she said.

"Oh, yeah? Then tell me what you think of when I say 'Hong Kong.'"

"The orchids," Marcie answered. "All the flowers are incredible, but there are *ninety* different kinds of orchid."

Ah, a lovely floral fact. A sensitive tycoon.

"Marcie, I will buy you one of every kind."

"I'll hold you to it."

"Anything to make you hold me," I replied.

New Year is icumen in, loudly sing Kung Fu!
I was dancing through the office, closing files and shaking
hands. For tomorrow we'd be heading for the East horizon.

"Don't worry," said Anita. "I'll burn candles in your pencil
box. *Aloha,* Oliver."

"No, no, Anita, get it right," replied the newly venerable sage
of Chinese culture. "*Kung hei fat choy.*"

"Are you suggesting that I've put on weight?"

"Ah, no, Anita," sage replied. "Meaning was our Chinese New
Year's wish: *Kung hei fat choy*—prosperity and happiness. Farewell."

"Farewell, you lucky bastard."

Thus we took off.

I don't remember much about Hong Kong. Except it was the last
time I saw Marcie Binnendale.

We departed Tuesday morning from New York, and stopped
just once—in Fairbanks—to refuel. I was anxious to try Baked
Alaska on the scene. Marcie wanted to go out and have a snowball fight. Before we could decide, they called us back on board.

We slept as best as possible across three seats. In our festive mood, we joined what swingers call the Mile-High Club. Which means we furtively made love while other passengers enjoyed Clint Eastwood gunning down innumerable baddies for a fistful of dollars.

It was early Wednesday (!) evening when we touched down in Tokyo. We had four hours to change planes. I was so zonked from twenty hours of assorted flying that I not-too-ceremoniously crashed right on a couch in Pan Am's Clipper Lounge. Meanwhile Marcie, ever effervescent, had a conference with some guys who'd come to meet her from the city. (This was in our deal; she'd have four days of duties, then we would take two weeks of screw-the-world vacation.) By the time she woke me for the final leg, she'd worked out all details for exchanging chic boutiques with Takashimaya, the Japanese purveyors of consumer elegance.

I slept no further. I was too excited, looking forward to the lights of Hong Kong Harbor. At last they sparkled into view as we descended just about the midnight hour. It was even better than the pictures I had seen.

John Alexander Hsiang was there to meet us. Clearly he is Number One for Marcie's matters in the Colony. He was late thirtyish, his outfit British and his accent U.S.A. ("I went to B-School in the States," he said.) He punctuated everything with "A-okay." Which did indeed describe all the arrangements he had made.

For, less than twenty minutes after we had landed, we were crossing Hong Kong Harbor from the airport to Victoria, where we'd be staying. The conveyance was a helicopter. And the view spectacular. The city was a diamond in the darkened China Sea.

"Local proverb," John Hsiang said. "'A million lights shall glow.'"

"How come they're up so late?" I asked.

"Our New Year festival."

You asshole, Barrett! You forgot why you were coming! You even knew it was the Year of the Dog!

"What time will everybody go to bed?"

"Oh, maybe two, three days." Mr. Hsiang smiled.

"I could last about another fifteen seconds," Marcie sighed.

"You mean you're tired?" I remarked, amazed that Wonder Woman would confess such things.

"Enough to cancel tennis in the morning," she replied. And kissed my ear.

I couldn't see the outside of the villa in the dark. But it was lush as Hollywood within. The place was halfway up the Peak. Which meant almost a mile above the harbor (higher than our 'copter flew), and so the backyard vista was incredible.

"Too bad it's winter. Just a bit too cold for swimming," John remarked. I hadn't even noticed that the garden had a pool.

"My head is swimming, John," I said.

"Why *don't* they have the fashion show in summer?" Marcie asked. We were simply chatting while the staff (an *amah* and two houseboys) brought in our stuff, unpacked and hung it up.

"Hong Kong summers aren't very pleasant," John replied. "Humidity is quite uncomfortable."

"Yeah, over eighty-five percent," said Barrett, who had done his homework. And was now awake enough to quote from it.

"Yes," said Mr. Hsiang. "Like August in New York."

Evidently John was loath to grant that anything in Hong Kong wasn't "A-okay."

"Good night. I hope you will enjoy our city."

"Oh, no question," I replied with grand diplomacy. "It is a many-splendored thing."

He left. No doubt enthusiastic at my literary reference.

Marce and I just sat, too far beyond fatigue to go to bed. Houseboy Number One provided wine and orange juice.

"Who owns this pleasure dome?" I asked.

"A landlord. We just rent it by the year. We've got a lot of people coming in and out. It's more convenient if we keep a place."

"What do we do tomorrow?" I inquired.

"Well, in just about five hours, a car will come to take me to our offices. Then scintillating luncheon with the Moguls of Finance. You could join us. . . ."

"Thanks. I'll pass."

"John will be at your disposal. You can see the sights with him. The Tiger Gardens, markets. Maybe you could spend the afternoon out on an island."

"Just with John?"

She smiled. "I'd like to have him show you Shatin."

"Yes, the monastery of ten thousand Buddhas. Right?"

"Right," she said. "But you and I will go to the Lan Tao Island by ourselves and spend the night there in the Polin monastery."

"Hey. You really know this place."

"I've been here many times," she said.

"Solo?" I inquired, unable to disguise my jealousy. I wanted this entire trip to be our special property.

"Not just by myself," she answered, "desperately alone. The sunsets do that to you."

Good. She was a neophyte to sharing sunsets. I would teach her that.

Tomorrow.

Naturally, I bought a camera.

John transported me next morning to Kowloon and in the massive Ocean Terminal I got loads of photographic apparatus at a steal.

"How do they do it, John?" I asked. "The Japanese equipment is cheaper than in Japan. The French perfume is cheaper than in Paris!" (I was buying Marcie some.)

"That is the secret of Hong Kong." He smiled. "This is a magic city."

First I had to see the flower markets in their New Year glory. Choy Hung Chuen, exploding with chrysanthemums and fruits and golden paper images. A technicolor banquet for my newly purchased lens. (And I bought a big bouquet for Marcie.)

Then back to Victoria. The ladder streets. A narrow San Francisco and a spiderlike bazaar. We went to Cat Street, where the vendors in the red-draped booths hawked *everything*—the wildest potpourri imaginable.

I ate a hundred-year-old egg. (I chewed and swallowed trying to avoid a taste.)

John did explain that actually these eggs take only weeks to make.

"They treat them with arsenic and they cover them with mud." (This after I had swallowed!)

We passed the herbalists. But I could not be tempted by the seeds or fungi or the dried sea horses.

Then the wineshops selling . . . pickled snakes.

"No, John," I said, "not pickled snakes."

"Oh, it is very useful," he replied, enjoying my dismay at the exotic. "Venom mixed with wine is very popular. It works wonders."

"For example . . . ?"

"Good for rheumatism. Also as an aphrodisiac."

Hopefully I needed neither at the moment.

"I'll keep that in mind," I said, "but now I've had it for today."

And then he drove me to the villa.

"If you can get ready in the early morning," John remarked as we pulled up, "I can show you something interesting. Of sport."

"Oh, I'm into sports."

"I'll pick you up at seven, then, okay? There's shadowboxing in the Botanical Gardens. Very fascinating."

"A-okay," I said.

"Have a lovely evening, Oliver," he said in parting.

"Thanks."

"Actually, it's lovely every evening in Hong Kong," he added.

"Marcie, it's a goddamn dream," I said.

Half an hour later we were on the water. As the sun was sinking. We were riding in a junk to Aberdeen, the "Floating Restaurants." Illumination everywhere.

"The proverb says a million lights," Miss Binnendale replied. "We've only started, Oliver." We dined by lantern glow on fish that had been swimming till we chose them. And I tried some wine from—are you watching, CIA?—Red China. It was pretty good.

The setting was so storybook, our text inevitably was banal. Like what the hell she did all day. (I'd been reduced to "Wow" and "Look at that.")

She had lunched with all the bureaucrats from Finance.

"They're so freaking *English*," Marcie said.

"It is a British colony, you know."

"But still—these characters' big dream is that Her Majesty will come to open their new cricket field."

"No shit. How jolly good. I bet she even does."

They brought dessert. We then discussed the Great Escape, now merely two days hence.

"John Hsiang is cute," I said, "and he's a stimulating guide. But I won't climb up Victoria till I can hold your hand on top."

"I'll tell you what. I'll meet you there tomorrow just to watch the sunset."

"Great."

"At five o'clock," she added, "at the peakest of the Peak."

"A toast to us with Commie wine," I said.

We kissed and floated.

How to fill the day till twilight on the top of Mount Victoria?

Well, first the shadowboxing. John knew every move. The sheer restraint of strength was just amazing. He then suggested that we see the jade collection at the Tiger Gardens and have *dim sum* lunch. I said okay, as long as there's no snakes.

Fifty-seven Kodacolor pictures later, we were drinking tea.

"What does Marcie do today?" I asked. I tried to make it

easier on John, who, after all, was an executive, not normally a tour guide.

"She's meeting with administrators for the factories," he said.

"Do Binnendale's own factories?"

"Not really 'own.' We simply have exclusive contracts. It's the vital factor in our operation. What we call the Hong Kong edge."

"What sort of edge?"

"The people. Or as you say it in the States, the people-power. U.S. workers get per day more than a Hong Kong man receives per week. Others even less . . ."

"What others?"

"Youngsters don't expect a grown-up's wage. They're very happy just with half. The end result's a lovely garment, f.o.b. New York, at a fraction of American or European price."

"I see. That's cool."

John seemed pleased that I had grasped the intricacies of the Hong Kong "edge." Frankly, people-power wasn't mentioned in the tourist office blurbs, so I was glad to learn.

"For example," John continued, "when two men want a single job, they can agree to split the wage. This way they both get work."

"No shit," I said.

"No shit." He smiled, appreciating my American vernacular.

"But that means each one works full time and gets half pay," I said.

"They don't complain," said Mr. Hsiang as he picked up the check. "Now, shall we take a drive into the country?"

"Hey, John, I'd like to see a factory. Would that be possible?"

"With thirty thousand in Hong Kong, it's very possible. They range from fairly big to family size. What would you like?"

"Well, how about a mini-tour of Marcie's?"

"A-okay with me," he said.

The first stop was a Kowloon neighborhood you'd never find on any Hong Kong postcard. Crowded. Dingy. Almost sunless.

We had to honk our way through mobs of people clogging up the street.

"Station Number One," said John after we'd parked inside a courtyard. "Making shirts."

We walked inside.

And suddenly I found myself back in the nineteenth century. In Fall River, Massachusetts.

It was a sweatshop.

There is no other goddamn word. It was a sweatshop.

Cramped and dark and stuffy.

Crouched over sewing machines were several dozen women working feverishly.

All was silent save for clicks and hums that signaled productivity.

Just exactly as it was in Amos Barrett's factories.

A supervisor scurried up to welcome John and me, the Occidental visitor. And then we toured. There was so much to see. The sights were maximal although the space was minimal.

The supervisor chattered in Chinese. John told me he was proud of how efficiently his ladies could produce the goods.

"The shirts they make here are terrific," John remarked.

He stopped and pointed to a female figure feeding shirt sleeves swiftly to the jaws of a machine.

"Look. Fantastic double-needle stitching. Highest quality. You just don't get that in the States these days."

I looked.

Sadly, John had picked a poor example. Not of workmanship, but of the worker.

"How old is this little girl?" I asked.

The moppet sewed on deftly, paying us no heed. If anything, she picked her pace up slightly.

"She fourteen," the supervisor said.

He evidently knew some English.

"John, that's utter bullshit," I said quietly. "This kid is ten at most."

"Fourteen," the supervisor parroted. And John concurred.

"Oliver, that is the legal minimum."

"I'm not disputing law, I'm simply saying this girl's ten years old!"

"She has card," the supervisor said. He had a working knowledge of the tongue.

"Let's see," I said. Politely. Though I didn't add a "please." John was impassive as the supervisor asked the little kid for her ID. She looked in panic. Christ, if only I could reassure her that it wasn't a bust.

"Here, sir."

The boss waved a card at me. It had no picture.

"John," I said, "it has no photograph."

"A picture's not required if you're under seventeen," he said.

"I see," I said.

They looked as if they wanted me to move on by.

"In other words," I then continued, "this kid's got an older sister's card."

"Fourteen!" the supervisor shouted once again. He gave the little girl her card back. Much relieved, she turned and started working even faster than before. But now taking furtive glances at me. Shit, suppose she hurts herself?

"Tell her to stay loose," I said to John.

He told her something in Chinese and she worked on, no longer glancing at me.

"Tea, please," said the supervisor, and he bowed us toward the cubicle that was his office.

John could see I hadn't bought the number.

"Look," he said, "she does a fourteen-year-old's job."

"And gets how much? You said they pay the 'youngsters' half."

"Oliver," said John, unruffled, "she takes home ten dollars every day."

"Oh, fine," I said, and added, "Hong Kong dollars. That's a *dollar-eighty*, U.S. bucks, correct?"

The supervisor handed me a shirt.

"He wants you to inspect the workmanship," said John.

"It's fine," I said. "That 'double stitching' stuff is really class (whatever that may be). In fact, I own a few of these myself."

You see, the shirts they made here bore the label **Mr. B.** And guys, it seems, are wearing them this year in sweater combinations.

As I sipped my tea, I wondered if a million miles away in old New York, Miss Elvy Nash knew *how* they made those fine-as-wine creations she was pushing.

"Let's go," I said to John.

I needed air.

I changed the conversation to the weather.

"It must be pretty brutal in the summer months," I said.

"Very humid," John replied.

We had run this gamut, so I knew the right riposte.

"Just like New York in August, huh?"

"About," he said.

"Does it . . . slow the ladies any?"

"Beg your pardon?"

"I didn't notice air conditioning back there," I said.

He looked at me.

"This is Asia, Oliver," he said, "not California."

And on we drove.

"Is your apartment air-conditioned?" I inquired.

John Hsiang looked at me again.

"Oliver," he calmly said, "here in the Orient the worker lives with different expectations."

"Really?"

"Yes."

"But don't you think that even here in Asia, John, the average worker's expectation is to have enough to *eat?*"

He didn't answer.

"So," I then continued, "you agree a dollar-eighty's not enough to live on, right?"

I knew his thoughts had long ago karate-chopped me dead.

"People work much harder here," he stated very righteously. "Our ladies don't read magazines in beauty parlors."

I sensed that John was conjuring up his private image of my mother lazing underneath a dryer.

"For example," he then added. "The young girl you saw. Her whole family works there. And her mother does some extra sewing for us in the evening."

"At her house?"

"Yes," John replied.

"Oh," I said. "What labor law calls 'homework,' right?"

"Right."

I waited for a sec.

"Johnny, you're a B-School graduate," I said. "You should recall why 'homework' is illegal in the States."

He smiled. "You don't know Hong Kong law."

"Come on, you fucking hypocrite!"

He slammed the brakes and skidded to a stop.

"I don't have to take abuse," he said.

"You're right," I answered, and I opened up the door. But damn, before I stormed away I had to make him *hear* the answer.

"Homework is illegal," I said softly, "'cause it gets around the union wage. Guys who have to work like that get paid whatever the employer cares to give them. Which is generally zilch."

John Hsiang glared at me.

"Oration over, Mr. Liberal?" he inquired.

"Yes."

"Then listen for a change and learn the local facts of life. They don't join unions here 'cause people *want* to split their pay and people *want* their kids to work and people *want* the chance to take some pieces home. You *dig?*"

I wouldn't answer.

"And for your goddamn lawyer information," John concluded, "there is *no* minimum wage in Hong Kong Colony. Now go to hell!"

He gunned away before I could inform him I already *was* there.

35

The explanations for the things we do in life are many and complex. Supposedly mature adults should live by logic, listen to their reason. Think things out before they act.

But then they maybe never heard what Dr. London told me once. Long after everything was over.

Freud—yes, Freud himself—once said that for the little things in life we should, of course, react according to our reason.

But for really big decisions, we should heed what our unconscious tells us.

Marcie Binnendale was standing eighteen hundred feet above the Hong Kong harbor. It was twilight. And the candles of the city were beginning to be lit.

The wind was cold. It blew the hair across her forehead in the manner I had often found so beautiful.

"Hi, friend," she said. "Look down at all those lights. We can see everything from here."

I didn't answer.

"Want me to indicate the points of interest?"

"I saw enough this afternoon. With Johnny."

"Oh," she said.

Then gradually she noticed I had not returned her smile of welcome. I was looking up at her, wondering was this the woman I had almost . . . loved?

"Something wrong?" she asked.

"Everything," I answered.

"For instance?"

I said it quietly.

"You've got little children working in your sweatshops."

Marcie hesitated for a moment.

"Everybody does it."

"Marcie, that is no excuse."

"Look who's talking," Marcie answered calmly. "Mr. Barrett of the Massachusetts textile fortune!"

I was prepared for this.

"That's not the point."

"Like hell! They took advantage of a situation just the way the industry is doing here."

"A hundred years ago," I said, "I wasn't there to say it made me sick."

"You're pretty sanctimonious," she said. "Just who picked you to change the world?"

"Look, Marcie, I can't change it. But I sure as hell don't have to join it."

Then she shook her head.

"Oliver, this bleeding liberal number's just a pretext."

I looked at her and didn't answer.

"You want to end it. And you're looking for a good excuse."

I could've said I'd found a goddamn good one.

"Come on," she said, "you're lying to yourself. If I gave *everything* to charity and went to teach in Appalachia, you'd find some other reason."

I reflected. All I really knew was I was anxious to depart.

"Maybe," I allowed.

"Then why not have the balls to say you just don't like me?"

Marcie's cool was melting. She was not upset. Not angry. Yet not quite in full control of all her fabled poise.

"No. I like you, Marce," I said. "I just can't live with you."

"Oliver," she answered quietly, "you couldn't live with *anyone*. You're still so hung up on Jenny, you don't *want* a new relationship."

I could not respond. She really hurt me by evoking Jenny.

"Look, I know you," she continued. "All your 'deep involvement with the issues' is a great façade. It's just a socially acceptable excuse to keep on mourning."

"Marcie?"

"Yes?"

"You are a cold and heartless bitch."

I turned and started off.

"Wait, Oliver."

I stopped and looked around.

She stood there. Crying. Very softly.

"Oliver . . . I need you."

I did not reply.

"And I think you need me too," she said. For a moment I did not know what to do.

I looked at her. I knew how hopelessly alone she felt.

But therein lay the problem.

So did I.

I turned and walked down Austin Road. Not looking back.

Night had fallen.

And I wished the darkness could have drowned me.

"What is your opinion, Doctor?"

"I think lemon meringue."

Joanna Stein, M.D., reached out across the counter and then placed a piece of pie upon her tray. This and two stalks of celery would be her lunch. She'd just explained that she was on a diet.

"Pretty weird," I commented.

"I can't help it," she replied. "I'm a sucker for the really gooey stuff. The celery is for my conscience."

It was two weeks after I'd got back. I'd spent the first days feeling tired, then the next few feeling angry. Then, as if returning to square one, I just felt lonely.

With a difference.

Two years ago, my grief had overwhelmed all other feelings. Now I knew that what I needed was the company of someone. Someone nice. I wouldn't wait or wallow.

My only qualm in calling up Joanna Stein was having to concoct some bullshit to explain why I'd been out of touch so long.

She never asked.

When I telephoned, she merely indicated she was pleased to hear from me. I invited her to dinner. She suggested lunch right at the hospital. I leaped and here we were.

She had kissed me on the cheek when I arrived. Now, for once, I kissed her back. We asked each other how we'd been and gave replies with vague details. We'd both been working hard, extremely busy. And so forth. She asked about my lawyering. I told a Spiro Agnew joke. She laughed. We were at ease with one another.

Then I asked about her doctoring.

"I finish here in June, thank God."

"What then?"

"Two years in San Francisco. At a teaching hospital and at a living wage."

San Francisco is, I quickly calculated, several thousand miles from New York City. Oliver, you clod, don't fumble this one.

"California's great," I said, to stall for time.

My social calendar had called for weekending in Cranston. Maybe I could ask her to drive up with me, just friend-to-friend. She would get along with Phil. And it would be a chance to get things started.

Then my mind absorbed her comment on my last remark.

"It's not just California," Jo had answered. "There's a guy involved."

Oh. A guy. It stands to reason. Life goes on without you, Oliver. Or did you think she'd sit and pine?

I wondered if my face betrayed my disappointment.

"Hey, I'm glad to hear it," I replied. "A doctor?"

"Sure," she smiled. "Whom else would I encounter on this job?"

"Is he musical?" I asked.

"He barely cuts it on the oboe."

He clearly cuts it with Joanna.

That's enough of jealous prying, Oliver. Now show you're cool and change the subject.

"How's King Louis?"

"Crazier than ever," she replied. "They all send love and tell you any Sunday . . ."

No. I wouldn't want to meet the oboist.

"Great. I'll come sometime," I lied.

There was a little pause. I sipped my coffee.

"Hey, can I level with you, Oliver?" she whispered furtively.

"Sure, Jo."

"I'm embarrassed, but I'd . . . like another piece of pie."

Gallantly, I fetched her one, pretending it was for myself. Joanna Stein, M.D., expressed eternal gratitude.

Our hour soon was up.

"Good luck in San Francisco, Jo," I said in parting.

"Please keep in touch."

"Yeah. Sure," I said.

And I walked very slowly downtown to my office.

Three weeks later came a turning point.

After years of threatening to do so, Father actually turned sixty-five. They held a celebration in his office.

The shuttle I flew up on was an hour late because of snowy weather. By the time I entered, many had drunk deeply at the flowing punch bowls. I was in an undulating sea of tweed. Everyone was saying what a jolly fellow Father was. And soon they would be singing it.

I behaved. I talked to Father's partners and their families. First Mr. Ward, a friendly fossil, and his future-fossil children. Then to the Seymours, once a lively couple, now reduced to but a single melancholy topic: Everett, their only son, a helicopter pilot in Vietnam.

Mother stood at Father's side, receiving envoys from the far-flung Barrett enterprises. There was even someone from the textile workers' union.

I could easily distinguish him. Jamie Francis was the only guest who didn't wear a Brooks or J. Press suit.

"Sorry you were late," said Jamie. "Wish you coulda heard my speech. Look—the members all pitched in."

He pointed at the board room table, where a gold Eternamatic clock shone 6:15.

"Your father's a good man. You should be proud," continued Jamie. "I've sat around a table with him nearly thirty years and I can tell you that they don't come any better."

I just nodded. Jamie seemed intent on giving me a replay of his testimonial.

"Back in the fifties, all the owners ran like rats and set up plants down South. They left their people high and dry."

That's no exaggeration. New England mill towns nowadays are almost ghost towns.

"But your dad just sat us down and said, 'We're gonna stay. Now help us be competitive.'"

"Go on," I said, as if he needed prompting.

"We asked for new machinery. I guess no bank was nuts enough to finance him. . . ."

He took a breath.

"So Mr. Barrett put his money where his mouth was. Three million bucks to save our jobs."

My father never told me this. But then I'd never asked.

"Of course the pressure's really on him now," said Jamie.

"Why?"

He looked at me and spoke two syllables: "Hong Kong."

I nodded.

He continued. "And Formosa. And they're starting now in South Korea. What the hell!"

"Yeah, Mr. Francis," I replied, "that's wicked competition." As well I knew.

"I'd use stronger language if we weren't in your father's office. He's a really good man, Oliver. Not like—if you'll pardon me—some other Barretts."

"Yeah," I said.

"In fact," said Jamie, "I think that's why he's tried so damn hard to be fair to us."

Suddenly, I looked across the room and saw a wholly different person where my father had been standing. One who'd shared with me a feeling that I had never known he had.

But *unlike* me, had done much more than talk about it.

Justice triumphed in November.

After several seasons of our discontent, Harvard beat the ass off Yale in football. Fourteen–twelve. Decisive factors were the

Lord and our defensive unit. The first sent mighty winds to hamper Massey's throwing game; the second stalled a final Eli drive. All of us in Soldiers Field were smiling.

"That was fine," said Father as we drove to downtown Boston.

"Not just fine—fantastic!" I replied.

The surest sign of growing old is that you start to *care* about who wins the Harvard–Yale game.

But as I said, the crucial thing is that we won.

Father parked the car near State Street in his office lot.

And we headed toward the restaurant to feast on lobster and banalities.

He strode with vigor. For despite his age, he still rowed on the Charles five times a week. He was in shape.

Our conversation was conspicuously football-oriented. Father never had—and I sensed never would—asked me the fate of my relationship with Marcie. Nor would he broach the other subjects he assumed taboo.

And so I took to the offensive.

As we passed the offices of Barrett, Ward and Seymour, I said, "Father?"

"Yes?"

"I'd like to talk to you about . . . the Firm."

He glanced at me. He didn't smile. But it took every muscle in his body to restrain himself. Athlete that he was, he wouldn't break his stroke until he crossed the finish line.

This was no sudden whim. And yet I never told my father by what complicated paths I had arrived at the decision to be . . . part of things. For it had taken time to work it out.

Unlike my usual decisions, I had pondered every day (and night) since I'd returned from Father's party more than half a year ago.

To start with, I could never love New York again.

It's not a city to cure loneliness. And what I needed most was to belong. Somewhere.

And maybe it was not just that I came to see my family with different eyes. Maybe I just wanted to go home.

I've tried to be so many things so far, just to avoid confronting who I am.

And I am Oliver Barrett. The Fourth.

December 1976

I've been in Boston nearly five years now. I worked in tandem with my father till he left the firm. At first, I do confess, I missed the legal action. But the more I got involved, the more I found that what we do at Barrett, Ward and Seymour is important too. I mean the companies we help to float create new jobs. And that's a source of pride to me.

Speaking of employment, in Fall River all our mills are flourishing. Actually, the only setback that our workers suffered has been on the playing field.

Each summer at our picnic, Rank & File plays Management in softball. Since my drafting into service, Labor's tide of victories has been reversed. I'm batting .604 (yes, folks), with seven homers in four years. I think they're looking forward to my ultimate retirement.

The *Wall Street Journal* does not mention all the enterprises we have financed. One omission was Phil's Bake Shop . . . of Fort Lauderdale. The gray and cold of Cranston winters got to Phil, and Florida was just too tempting.

He calls me once a month. I ask about his social life, aware that there are many eligible ladies in his area. He ducks the question with a "Time will tell." And quickly turns the subject to *my* social life.

Which is pretty good. I live on Beacon Hill, that legendary

J 17

cornucopia of recent college graduates. It's not too difficult to make new friends. And not just business types. I often lift a glass with Stanley Newman, who's a jazz pianist. Or Gianni Barnea, a just-about-to-be-discovered painter.

And, of course, I'm still in touch with all my old friends. The Simpsons have a little son and Gwen is preg with number two. They stay with me when they're in Boston for a football game or something. (I've got lots of room.)

Steve reports Joanna Stein has married Martin Jaffe, who I gather is an ophthalmologist as well as an oboist. They're living on the Coast.

According to a little squib I read in *Time*, Miss Binnendale has recently re-wed. A guy named Preston Elder ("thirty-seven, Washington attorney").

I suppose the matrimony epidemic will eventually strike me. Of late I've seen a lot of Annie Gilbert, who's a distant cousin. At this point I can't say if it's serious.

Meanwhile, thanks to all those hockey fans who voted for me, I'm a Harvard Overseer. It's a good excuse to go to Cambridge and pretend I'm still what I no longer am. The undergraduates appear much younger and a trifle scruffier. But who am I to judge? My job obliges me to wear a tie.

So life is challenging. The days are full. I get a lot of satisfaction from my work. Yes, Barrett that I am, I get my rocks off on Responsibility.

I'm still in shape. I jog along the Charles each evening.

If I go five miles, I get to glimpse the lights of Harvard just across the river. And see all the places I had walked when I was happy.

I run back in the darkness, reminiscing just to pass the time.

Sometimes I ask myself what I would be if Jenny were alive.
And then I answer:
I would also be alive.